tied up
in you

tied up
in you

ERIN FLETCHER

Entangled Publishing, LLC
2614 South Timberline Road
Suite 109
Fort Collins, CO 80525
Visit our website at www.entangledpublishing.com.

Crush is an imprint of Entangled Publishing, LLC.

Edited by Heather Howland
Cover design by Heather Howland
Cover art from iStock

Manufactured in the United States of America

First Edition July 2017

Chapter One

MALINA

The doorbell rang.

I sighed and pushed aside my AP chem book. *It better not be someone selling something, unless that "something" is Thin Mint cookies.* But when I opened the door, there were no girls or boxes of chocolaty mint magic in sight.

Nope. Just a hot guy.

I leaned against the doorframe, trying to look bored when all I wanted to do was throw myself into his arms. "Hi."

"Hi," he echoed.

I tipped my head to one side and studied him—totally not a hardship, but I'd never tell him that. "Hmm. Do I know you?"

He grinned and held out a hand. "I'm Jackson. Luke Jackson, actually, but most people call me Jackson. Have you seen a girl named Malina Hall around? I hear she lives here."

Fighting back a smile, I shook his hand. "I'm Malina Hall. You know, it's funny. You look a lot like this guy I used to know."

"Oh, really? Good guy?" He stuck his thumbs in the front pockets of his jeans, his grin widening.

"Decent. He was my best friend, actually." I folded my arms over my chest. "But then he started playing for this really elite hockey team, and I never saw him anymore. Barely even heard from him."

His smile fell, and he looked at his feet, letting his long brown hair fall in front of his eyes. "He sounds kind of like a tool."

"Yeah, he kind of does," I said.

Jackson peered down at me. "For the record, he missed you. I mean, probably. He sounds like the kind of guy who would miss someone like you."

I couldn't hold back my smile anymore. "For the record, I missed him, too."

"Oh, thank God." He broke character and pulled me in for a hug so tight I could barely breathe. But when it came to Jackson, breathing was overrated. He wasn't the kind of guy any girl could breathe around, really. Even I wasn't immune.

We'd met back in fifth grade, when desks were assigned in alphabetical order and there were no last names in between "Hall" and "Jackson." I was the girl who had a case full of sharpened pencils for the endless times when he lost his. He was the guy who pitched to me gently during recess kickball games so I could get a kick, even though he was on the other team. Regardless of the fact that we were pretty much opposites, we stayed friends after that, bonding over school and scary movies and being there for each other during times like when his parents divorced or my grandma Tutu had a stroke.

Though everyone was off at some Monday night trivia game, I could practically hear my dad saying I was heating the cold fall air outside. I squirmed out of Jackson's grasp.

"C'mon. Dad would throw us out if he found out we were letting all the cold air in."

I stood to the side to let him pass, loving the warm scent of Jackson that was as familiar as Tutu's cooking. "Hey," I said, frowning. "Did you get taller? You've been gone, like, a month. How is it possible you got taller?"

He slipped off his shoes and headed over to his usual spot on our couch. "I don't know, but I think I'm six-one now. My pants are all too short again."

I marked my place in my chem book and set it on the coffee table so I could sit next to him. I'd finish my homework when he left. "Must be something in the water in...where were you this time? Alaska? Iceland? Antarctica?"

"Close," he said, chuckling. "Montreal. And Chicago before that, and Wisconsin before that."

"It's strange. Those all sound like places that get cell phone reception. Maybe even free wifi." I tried to keep my tone teasing. Jackson and I had started to grow apart the past year as he focused more on hockey and I focused more on school. It sucked, and I would have liked to hear from him a whole lot more than I did, but I also knew it was inevitable. Plus, I couldn't deny the fact that I got a lot more schoolwork and college stuff done when he wasn't around.

He dropped his head back against the well-worn couch. "You're right. I suck. I'm so busy with practices and games, and I'm doing a lot of cross-training, and by the time I'm done with all of that—"

"I know, I know." I nudged his shoulder with mine. "Just giving you a hard time."

Before he could respond, his stomach growled, loud and insistent. He grimaced. "I swear I ate like two hours ago."

Despite our growing apart, some things never changed, like the size of Jackson's appetite. I got up and headed toward the kitchen. "Come on. There are leftovers for you in the fridge."

In a split second, he was on his feet and behind me. "For me?" he asked hopefully. "Did you tell your family I was going to be back in town?"

I didn't look at him so he couldn't see my smile. "Maybe."

"That means yes, right? Did your mom and Tutu cook for me? Don't toy with me, Hall."

I opened the fridge and removed two containers of leftovers. One was covered in translucent plastic wrap so he could easily see the contents.

"*Laulau*?" he asked. "Oh my gosh. That looks amazing. Do you know how terrible food on the road is? Do you know how long I've been craving *laulau*? Days. Weeks. *Months*." He motioned to the Cool Whip container in my hand. It had been used, washed, and refilled so many times that one of the o's and the W had disappeared completely. "And is that…?"

I opened the "Col hip" tub, revealing its creamy purple contents. It was fresh enough to still be sweet—just the way Jackson liked it.

His face lit up. Everyone should be loved by someone as much as Luke Jackson loved food. "*Poi!*"

"Of course. I swear, Tutu reached for the taro the second she heard your name." My mom's side of the family was from Hawaii, and that was where she'd met my dad. Though she'd moved back to Dad's home of Michigan after he finished college, she'd still cooked us Hawaiian and Polynesian foods pretty often. All that Hawaiian goodness had only increased a few years ago when Tutu moved in with us.

Feeding my bottomless pit of a best friend was one of their favorite things to do.

"Grab whatever you want to drink," I said. I uncovered the *laulau* and stuck the container in the microwave. Though there were enough of the steamed pouches of pork in there to make two or three meals for me, Jackson would eat them all, plus probably sniff out the sweet coconut *haupia* on the bottom shelf of the fridge for dessert.

"How's Tutu?" he asked. He grabbed a glass from the cupboard above the sink and started filling it from the tap.

"She's good." I scooped some of the *poi* onto a plate for him, leaving plenty of room for the *laulau*. "Saw her neurologist last week, and I guess he said everything's good. My dad caught her trying to get the Christmas stuff out of the attic by herself the other day."

He laughed. "Of course she was. She still thinks she's, what, thirty?"

"If that. I thought my dad was going to explode."

"But wait, it's not even Thanksgiving and already she wants Christmas?"

"I think she and my mom would leave our Christmas tree up year round if my dad and I would let them." Christmas in Hawaii was a big deal. Even though there wasn't snow, there were surfing Santas, Christmas palm trees, beautiful poinsettias, festivals of lights, and the song "*Mele Kalikimaka*" played on repeat from Thanksgiving through the new year. Tutu and my mom did their best to bring that joy to the frigid, gray Michigan winters. The presence of Christmas decorations in November was normal at my house, and I wouldn't be surprised if Mom started asking trick-or-treaters to help hang a string of lights before they took their Halloween candy.

The microwave beeped, and I removed the container so I could flip the stuffed taro leaves. Jackson groaned and leaned over my shoulder. "Oh my gosh, that smells amazing."

I elbowed him in the stomach. "Quit drooling on me." I stuck the dish back into the microwave and turned it on again. "Speaking of drooling, how's Kristy-with-a-y?" I had to specify, because he'd also dated Kristie-with-an-ie not that long ago.

He downed his glass of water in a couple of quick swallows

and went to the sink to refill it. "Gross. She didn't drool on me. She was a little…overenthusiastic."

"If that's what you call the girl who painted your number on her face for your hockey *practice*, then okay. But wait, 'was?'"

"Yeah. Was. We broke up while I was in Wisconsin."

I put on my best sympathetic face. "Sorry."

He shrugged. "It's fine."

It wasn't a front. He was telling the truth. When most of my friends broke up with someone, it was the end of the world. The last time Izzy broke up with her girlfriend, the girl cried for *weeks*. When Jackson broke up with someone or started seeing someone new, it was about as newsworthy as Izzy getting busted for texting in class. Again.

"So who's the new girl?" The microwave beeped, and I took the *laulau* out, replacing it with his plate of *poi* to zap for a few seconds.

"There is no new girl."

The words almost made me drop the container I was holding. "I'm sorry, what?"

He laughed and removed a mismatched fork and knife from the silverware drawer. "I don't always have to be dating someone."

The microwave beeped again. "Of course *I* know that. I wasn't sure *you* did."

"I'm too busy with hockey to date anyone right now anyway."

I finished arranging the food and turned to present it to him. "True, but that's never stopped—" I cut myself off when he snatched the plate out of my hands, dunked a stuffed taro leaf in *poi*, and took a big bite.

"Hot, hot," he said, fanning his mouth with his silverware-holding hand in a way that made me nervous he'd fork his own eyeball.

"Serves you right," I said. "What, did you leave your manners in Canada?"

He chewed and swallowed, then smiled at me with a tiny piece of taro leaf in between his front teeth. "Sorry."

How any girl put up with him was beyond me. How *I* put up with him was beyond me, but seeing that leaf in his teeth reminded me of when we were in sixth grade and I had to get braces. Not only had Jackson threatened to punch anyone who made fun of me, but he'd also turned down all offers of gum, popcorn, and chewy candy for a year because he didn't want me to be the only one who couldn't have them. Manners or no manners, he was still my best friend. I rolled my eyes and nudged him toward the table, where he sat in his usual spot and I sat in mine.

"Better?" he asked when he was seated with a fork in one hand and a knife in the other.

"Much. I swear, being around a team of guys all the time makes you so uncivilized."

He ignored my comment and tore into his food. One of the *laulau* and most of the poi were gone within seconds.

"So good," he said. "I can't wait to thank Tutu and your mom."

"Hey, I helped," I said.

"Thank you, Malina." He took another bite so big I was grateful I'd taken a first aid class for babysitting that included the Heimlich maneuver.

I laughed. "Where do you *put* all of that food?"

"Behind my left kneecap," he said in between bites.

After the next bite, he grinned at me again. The fake tooth he'd gotten to replace the one he knocked out during a game a few years back was whiter than the rest. I'd forgotten that little detail.

"You know you missed me," he said.

"Yeah," I said. Because despite everything—the insatiable

appetite and lack of manners and slacking on keeping in touch, and the fact that we were growing apart as we grew up and our priorities changed and clashed—I did miss my best friend. "Very much."

Chapter Two

JACKSON

"I ate too much," I groaned as I sat down on the couch next to Malina. I put my feet up on the coffee table, where the edge was worn smooth by years of people sitting in this exact position.

"I warned you to stop after the first square of *haupia*," she said, poking me in the stomach.

It didn't hurt, but I moaned dramatically for effect anyway. "But it was so good."

"Glad you liked it." She ran a hand through her dark hair. It had gotten longer since the last time I saw her. It was well below her shoulders. I liked it.

I nudged my toe against the giant textbook that sat on the coffee table. "How's school?"

"Boring without you," she said. "But I aced my last calculus exam."

"Of course you did," I said. "Good work."

"Will you be back in class tomorrow?"

My body gave an involuntary shudder at the thought of being back at school in a few short hours. The biggest benefit to joining USA Hockey's National Team Development Program—besides the hockey, of course—was that I got to replace school with a tutor during travel times. It wasn't that I was terrible at school; it just wasn't my thing. One day in sixth grade, when Malina and I had the world's longest math homework assignment, she resorted to motivating me with candy. For each problem I solved, she'd slide an M&M across the table to me. I ended up with a sugar high, a rainbow-colored tongue, and a stomachache, but I finished the assignment. I wondered if I was too old for that kind of thing now. "I guess. I'm in town for the next three weeks or some ridiculously long time period like that. Not many games, and none on the road."

"No hockey travel, no girlfriend... What are you going to do with all of your free time?"

I smiled. "Eat all of your food, work out, and sleep."

She laughed. "And school."

"If I must." Something in the corner of the living room caught my eye. "How goes the project?" I got up to inspect it, trying to remember what it looked like the last time I'd been over.

The project was a model of the solar system she'd been working on for over a year. Even though it was a science project, it looked like art, with the sun and each planet made out of swirled glass with a light inside. The sun was the anchor, and each of the planets rotated around it on arms that showed the distance from the sun. She'd started working on it as a STEM thing last year and was planning on entering it in our school's competition this year. When she won there like I knew she would, she'd go on to regional competitions, where she'd win it all.

Malina sighed and walked over to stand next to

me. "Progress is stalled." The words were heavy with disappointment.

I toyed with one of the planets, making it spin around its axis. Venus, maybe? The fact that I could barely name the planets while she could make something like this said a lot about the two of us. "What happened?"

"Problems with the app that controls it," she said. "Or that's *supposed* to control it, anyway."

"You'll figure it out."

She sighed and walked back to the couch. "I'm not sure I will. And even if I do, it won't be fast enough."

Leaving Venus alone, I returned to my seat. "When is the deadline for the school competition?"

"In a couple of weeks, which probably isn't enough time to figure it out. Especially not when I have midterms coming up and about a million scholarship applications due between now and then."

"But if you make it to the bigger competitions, you can earn scholarship money that way, right?"

"Yeah."

The pause before she said it was just long enough to let me know she doubted herself. I kicked myself that I hadn't done a better job of keeping in touch while I was on the road. If there was anyone who could sniff out Malina's self-doubt and tear it to shreds, it was me. It was just that sometimes it was easier to avoid thinking about home when I was several states or countries away. It made the distance sting less.

"You'll figure it out. You're the smartest person I know. Someday, when you're a famous astrophysicist who has her own galaxy named after her, I'll say, 'I remember when she thought she couldn't finish her STEM project. Now look at her. She's changing the universe.'"

Normally, Malina would find something to correct me about. That galaxies aren't named after people or the universe can't actually be changed or something else that she geeked out about and I'd never understand. But she just frowned.

Okay, so she didn't want to talk about it. That could be a conversation for another day. Today was for catching up and talking about things that wouldn't make Malina sad. "Hey, did you watch the last episode of *The Haunting*?"

Her face lit up at the mention of our favorite series. I'd missed that—her enthusiasm over every little thing, including TV.

"Yes! Oh my gosh, I loved—"

"The new character? Donovan?"

"Yes!"

Even though I'd been watching from my nine thousandth hotel room of the year, hundreds of miles from home, I'd been thinking about Malina the whole time, knowing she'd love every second of it. "I knew you would. What about the part where Malachi busted into that abandoned cemetery? Be honest. You had to cover your eyes, didn't you?"

She scoffed at me. "No."

I raised my eyebrows. The chances of her becoming *that* brave during the time we'd been apart were about the same as my chances of switching from hockey to baseball and getting drafted straight to the major leagues.

She sighed. "Fine. Yes. I covered my face with a pillow for that scene, okay?"

Normally, I'd rib her over something like that, but I couldn't. Not this time. "It scared the shit out of me, too. I jumped and knocked over a can of pop. Spilled all over the hotel carpet."

"Oops."

"Yeah, oops. Hey, do you remember that time we went on the haunted hayride freshman year?"

She gasped. "When Cory Hammond screamed like a girl and peed his pants? Yeah, I remember."

I smiled. Telling stories from my past to my teammates or whatever girl I was seeing was fine, but it wasn't the same as being with the person who'd lived those memories, too. "Poor guy never did quite rebound from that. But it was a fun night."

"Hey, the only reason I didn't cry and pee *my* pants was because I hid behind you the whole time."

I remembered that—the feeling of her tucked against my back, between my shoulder blades. I'd been dating someone else at the time, holding someone else's hand, but that hadn't mattered. Protecting was what best friends did.

"Can we watch that *Haunting* episode again?" I asked. "I think I need to see it one more time to prepare for the next episode."

She hesitated.

"I won't even complain if you cover your eyes for the cemetery scene," I said.

"It's not that. I just haven't finished my homework yet."

"Oh, come on. It's probably homework that isn't even due tomorrow, right?"

She sighed. "Do you have to know everything all the time?"

"As a matter of fact, I do." I got up to turn off the lights, leaving us in the near pitch black, except for dim light coming from the kitchen down the hall. Within seconds, I'd pulled up Netflix on her TV and burrowed into the couch. Before joining the NTDP team, I'd spent more time in that exact spot than I could count. That couch, right there with Malina, no worries about hockey or girls or anything else…it was perfect. How had I forgotten how much I had missed this? How did I always forget?

Next to me, Malina sighed as she tucked her legs up under her. "I am totally Team Donovan."

"See? Watching this again is better than doing homework, right?"

"Maybe," she said, but her eyes were glued to the screen.

"Say it."

"Say what?"

"Say, 'You were right, Luke.'"

When she looked at me, there was a sparkle in her dark eyes from the glow of the TV. "Not in a million years, Luke."

I reached for her side. There was a ticklish spot right above her left hip that I'd discovered sometime during our freshman year. Not many people knew about it, but a few quick tickles in that spot and she'd be a giggling mess of putty in my hands, guaranteeing she'd admit I was right.

"Don't!" she squealed when my hand was still inches away. "Okay, okay! You're right! You're right! This is absolutely better than doing homework."

At the last second, I let my hand drop back to the couch.

"Mean," she said.

"What? I didn't actually tickle you."

"No, but you—" She cut herself off when there was a scream from one of the characters. "Oh, cemetery scene!" she said, turning and burying her head in my shoulder.

"Wimp," I said, but let her hide there. Her hair smelled familiar and sweet, like mangoes.

"You said you wouldn't make fun of me!" she protested, but didn't turn her head.

"Just kidding."

There was a loud *bang* and the crash of shattering glass, but it wasn't on the TV. My heart jumped from my chest to my throat. The noise came from somewhere down the hall. The kitchen window? The back door? Was someone breaking into the house?

Holy shit.

Malina's head whipped up and she clutched my arm hard enough that she probably would have drawn blood if I hadn't been wearing long sleeves. "What was that?" she whispered.

"I don't know," I said, prying her hand from my arm and giving it a squeeze that I hoped was more assuring than shaky. "Stay here."

Someone on the TV screamed and I nearly jumped out of my skin. Stupid show. I flicked the flashlight on my phone and focused on holding it steady as I walked toward the kitchen. Maybe I could sympathize with Cory Hammond and his bladder back on that haunted hayride after all.

The single lightbulb over the sink wouldn't be bright enough for me to see everything, but it was enough that I'd hopefully be able to grab a knife, or grab Malina and get the hell out of there.

I peeked around the corner and into the kitchen, expecting to see the window in a million pieces, or someone wearing all black and looking for something to steal. Nothing seemed out of place, but it was still dark.

I mentally counted to three and flicked on the rest of the overhead lights, my pulse as fast as it would be if I'd just done wind sprints on the ice.

Nothing. No broken window. No thief.

"Jackson?" Malina called from the couch.

"Shh," I insisted. Glass broke. We both *heard* it. So where was the bad guy? Skulking around the back of the house? I hesitated. Grabbing Malina and throwing her in my car was sounding better and better. Why hadn't I brought a hockey stick in?

I was about to sneak through the kitchen, toward the laundry room and the back door, when something caught my eye.

Light, sparkling off something in the sink.

Relief nearly melted me into a puddle on the floor. *Oh thank God*. There wasn't an intruder, just the glass I'd used at dinner that had slipped off the drying rack and shattered in the sink. I opened the cupboard with the garbage can, carefully tossed the pieces inside, and then rinsed away any remaining shards. When I was sure Malina wouldn't cut herself reaching for something in the sink, I flicked off the lights and returned to the living room.

"What happened?" she asked.

I sat back in my place on the couch. "Apparently, we're not as good at dish-stacking Jenga as we thought we were."

She breathed a relieved sigh and let her head drop back onto my shoulder. "That's all it was? A dish broke?"

"The glass I used for water. It's toast. Sorry."

"It's fine. God, I really thought someone was breaking in or—" She cut herself off.

I grinned. Knowing what Malina was going to say before she said it was one of my skills. It was pretty obvious what embarrassing place her brain was going. "Or what?"

"Nothing. Never mind."

"Or the ghost from *The Haunting* made its way from the screen and into your kitchen?"

"Come on, you were scared, too."

I laughed. "Yeah, I was for a second."

"Well, thank you for coming to my rescue. I like you even better than Donovan."

She curled back up against me. God, I'd missed this. I'd missed *her*.

"Hey, Jackson?"

I meant to say, "Yeah?" That would have been the normal, reasonable thing to do. Instead, I turned and suddenly my face was inches from hers. I didn't move. I barely breathed. I *missed* her.

Then, almost as if my brain wasn't attached to my body, I tipped her chin up and pressed my lips to hers. Everything slipped away—the show in the background, the broken glass in the kitchen, the fact that I was kissing my best friend. My whole world narrowed to the feeling of her soft lips on mine, the jolts of pleasure it sent from my brain to my toes and everywhere in between, and the sweet taste of sugar and coconut. I reached for her face, her hair, wanting to pull her closer, needing more, and—

"What the hell?" Malina gasped, jerking backward.

My hand froze awkwardly in midair as reality slammed into me. Oh, shit. *Shit. I kissed my best friend.* "Sorry," I said, jumping up and slamming my leg on the coffee table. "Ow," I moaned as I turned on the lamp, then turned on the overhead light for good measure.

The look on Malina's face was one I hadn't seen before. Her eyes were wide with something—shock? Disgust? Embarrassment?

My cheeks and ears burned. Was it possible for your nose to blush? I was pretty sure mine was. "Malina, I'm so sorry. I was just…" I ran a hand through my hair, struggling to come up with something, *anything* I could say to excuse what had happened. "I was just so relieved there wasn't a serial killer or something in the kitchen, and I just…" Nope. There weren't any more words. There were hundreds of thousands of words in the English language and not one of them was going to help me.

For a long time, she didn't say anything. A *long* time. The expression on her face didn't change. Then she nodded slowly. "Right. Yeah. I was relieved, too."

She was going to accept my ridiculously lame excuse? Or at least pretend to accept it? "Right? Yeah. Okay. Sorry."

She frowned. "Just…don't. Do that. Ever. Again."

"No," I said quickly. Spastically quickly. Oh God, my cheeks were still on fire. I couldn't look her in the eyes. "Sorry. I won't. It won't happen again. I should probably go." Then I winced and said, "Ow," when I took a step that jarred my bruised leg.

Her frown changed from confusion to concern. "Are you

okay?"

"Yeah," I said, too quickly again. "Fine. Just…bruised my leg. Banged it. I'll be fine."

"Do you need some ice?"

"No. No. I'm fine. Sorry again. Thanks for dinner. I'll see you at school, right? Sorry." Instead of coming out like individual sentences, the words kind of blurred together into one big blob of awkward.

Malina got up and walked me to the door. "Yeah. I'll see you at school."

I had one foot out the door when she stopped me.

"Jackson?"

As much as I wanted to keep going, I couldn't ignore her. I stopped and turned and looked somewhere in the vicinity of her left shoulder. Not in her eyes. Not at her lips or her boobs. Shoulders were safe. "Yeah?"

"I don't really know what just happened, but it was an accident. We're still friends. It's fine."

I forced a nod and kept my eyes on her shoulder. "Okay. Thank you. Sorry. Good night."

When I got in my car, I leaned back against the headrest and tried to breathe. Despite what she said, it *wasn't* okay. I'd kissed my best friend. I'd acted like an idiot who didn't know how to human, not the confident hockey player who kissed girls all the time.

But the worst part? Worse than the kiss or the embarrassment or awkwardness that followed?

I *liked* kissing Malina.

A lot.

I was screwed.

Chapter Three

It was *fine*? As soon as Jackson pulled away, I scrambled back inside and leaned against the front door, pretty certain the cold wood was the only thing keeping me on my feet. I'd said it was fine because it was the only thing I could think to say, or maybe because I wanted it to be true. I knew it wasn't. What happened wasn't *fine*. It was…I couldn't even *process* what it was.

I closed my eyes as swirling thoughts made my vision swirl, too. We'd just been sitting on the couch, watching TV like we had a thousand times before, and yeah, the "someone maybe trying to break in" thing was new, but that didn't mean anything. Why had he *kissed* me? My hands started to go numb, like my heart was pumping too much blood to my brain in an effort to figure this out to bother with my fingers.

"Malina?"

When I looked up, my mom was standing in front of me with her coat in her hand, frowning. They must have just gotten home and come in through the garage. "Oh," I said, but my voice cracked and I had to clear my throat before I could say anything else. "Hi."

"I thought you said Luke was going to be here." When I didn't respond right away, her frown deepened. "Are you okay?"

Oh, God. Could she tell Jackson had kissed me? Was there some kind of visible evidence on my lips? Was there a "my best friend's mouth was on mine" expression that I didn't know about and therefore didn't know how to hide?

"He..." I fumbled for a white lie. "You just missed him. He had to do something for his family. But he said thank you for dinner."

"That boy ate all the *laulau*?" Tutu called.

I used that distraction to escape my mom's scrutiny. I pushed away from the door and forced my legs to cooperate as I walked toward the kitchen. Thoughts about Jackson—or really, staring into space not knowing what to think about Jackson—could wait. "I told you he would, didn't I?"

Mom followed me into the kitchen, where Tutu was slicing the remaining *haupia*. She put a square on the plate and handed it to my dad.

"*Mahalo*," Dad said. His Hawaiian pronunciation wasn't as good as Tutu's, but it was so much better than mine.

"You're welcome. Malina?"

I shook my head at her offer of dessert. If there was one thing I was sure of, it was that I wasn't hungry. "How was trivia?"

"Good," Mom said. "We lost, but it was fun. Lots of teams tonight."

The three adults took seats at the kitchen table while they ate. Instead of taking my own seat, I leaned against Tutu's chair. She patted my arm a few times, her rich caramel skin warm against my own, giving me the reassurance I didn't realize I needed.

"Lots of *good* teams tonight," Mom said. "We need to up our game."

"Or we need a ringer," Dad said. "Speaking of game, how's hockey going for Jackson? I saw the team's doing better than they were earlier this season."

My stomach flipped. Obviously my family wasn't going to make this any easier.

"He seems fine," I said, trying to keep my voice even. "They're home for a few weeks."

"Oh, good," Mom said. "I know you've missed seeing him at school."

School. In less than twelve hours. I was going to have to see Jackson at school in less than twelve hours. I had to go figure out what in the world I was going to do. "Speaking of school, I should get some homework done."

"Don't work too hard, my *mo'opuna*," Tutu said.

"She has to work hard," Dad said. "Gotta keep that GPA up so she can get into a school with a good business program, right?"

Thoughts of Jackson drifted away as my heart sank. The rational part of my brain knew that path would lead to a solid future. But the rest of my brain—and my heart, apparently— were having a hard time letting go of the applications I hadn't sent in to schools with astrophysics programs.

Those schools seemed like a good idea back in middle school when I learned people could make a living studying stars and planets and everything space-related—things I did for fun when I had free time. But I wasn't a naive middle schooler anymore. Not everyone could grow up to be ballerinas or firemen or doctors, and while my dream was different from the rest of my classmates, it was still just that. A dream.

"Right," I said, and hoped my family wouldn't pick up on

my lack of enthusiasm. "Don't worry. I'm working hard."

"We know you are," Mom said.

"Did you look over those interview questions I sent to you?" Dad asked. "The big day is only a couple weeks away."

"The big day" was the day of a scholarship interview with my dad's company. Even if my dad didn't work there, I still had a decent shot since I'd been an intern in the office the past two summers. My dad had been quick to point out that many scholarship recipients had gone on to have long and impressive careers within the car industry—his company, specifically. He'd also been quick to send some sample questions that he claimed he got from Google, but I wouldn't have been shocked if he'd bribed them straight out of the scholarship interviewers themselves.

"Not yet," I said. "But I will."

"Good. You should have your answers memorized. You'll have a better shot if you sound confident."

"What your dad means to say," Mom said, getting up to clear empty plates from the table, "is that we know you'll do great, and we'll be proud of you no matter what happens." She gave him a pointed look.

He gave me a sheepish grin. "Right. What she said."

"Thanks," I said, even though the words didn't come anywhere close to making me feel better. "I'll be upstairs if you need me."

I headed to the living room to pick up my books on the way to my bedroom. It wasn't the room where I'd spent most of my childhood. *That* room currently belonged to Tutu. My new room was smaller and didn't even have a closet. My bed took up most of the space, and I always stubbed my toe on the dresser that took up the rest, but it had a big window, and there was enough room on the walls for the space artwork I'd collected, so that was all that mattered. The only thing I wished there was room for was my STEM project, but having an unfinished project in my bedroom might stress me out too much to sleep.

Stress. The churning feeling in my stomach made it pretty clear I was going to have to deal with some of that before I could focus on my AP chem homework. Like any good scientist, I turned to the scientific method.

Question: How do I get over kissing my best friend?

Hypothesis: ~~Change my name, skip school for the rest of the year, and avoid hockey rinks like the plague.~~ Pretend it didn't happen.

Experiment: Look for evidence that the kiss was a mistake:

> - Our evening had been perfectly normal right up until he kissed me.

> - The glass-in-the-kitchen scare made him do something he normally wouldn't do.

> - Jackson was a playboy who had kissed almost every girl in our school.

> - He was also a distraction, as evidenced by the fact that I was sitting here thinking about him instead of doing my homework.

Analysis: The kiss was definitely a mistake.

Conclusion: Pretend it didn't happen. Don't let it be a distraction.

With determination, I opened my textbook and continued working on my homework. I managed to stay focused and had nearly finished the assignment when my phone buzzed. As much as I tried to ignore it, I could see Jackson's name on the screen, along with the silly selfie he'd snapped one day last year when we were hanging out and I left my phone unattended. *Just a mistake. Don't let it be a distraction.*

I sighed and turned back to my textbook, but when I read the same paragraph for the third time without understanding a word of it, my emotions won the battle with my mind. The phone felt weird as I picked it up, like it weighed too much or too little or somehow both at the same time. Why was I nervous about a text from Jackson?

Jackson: *Hey…are we still okay?*

The scientist in me had proven that we were.

Me: *We're fine. I know it was an accident.*

Me: *By the way, I never thanked you for rescuing me from the broken glass of doom.*

He sent the thumbs up emoji.

Jackson: *You're welcome.*

Jackson: *Am I interrupting your homework again?*

I sent the book emoji.

Jackson: *Sorry. I'll let you get back to it. See you tomorrow.*

Me: *See you then.*

When I set my phone down, a thought kept pinging at the back of my brain. Despite my analysis, despite the many facts that said the kiss was a mistake, there was one fact I'd been trying to ignore but couldn't anymore: I'd *liked* the kiss. Yes, it had caught me completely off guard, but that was the only negative thing about it. Everything else…the softness of his lips against mine, the way we fit together like it was meant to be, the warmth his mouth left behind, the tingles that made me shiver when he pulled away…

That was the kind of science that proved I was in big trouble. But as I stared up at an old poster that still showed Pluto as one of the planets, I let myself hope that this might be one time when science was wrong.

Chapter Four

When my alarm went off the next morning, I groaned. First, it was a school day. Second, it was a school day after weeks of travel, which meant I wasn't used to times before six a.m. Third, I'd had a dream about Malina. Not the "hanging out with my best friend" kind of dream. The *other* kind. It made for a truly love/hate relationship with my subconscious. It also made me dread seeing her despite the text she'd sent saying we were okay. We *were* okay, or we would be, as long as I could keep my brain where it belonged.

When I got to school, after complaining to my mom that she really needed to restock the fridge now that I was home again, I headed to the cafeteria. Meeting Malina there had been our tradition since freshman year, sometimes with a couple of other friends or the people we were dating, sometimes just the two of us, depending on who got to school when. But we always met. I wasn't about to ruin that tradition. This would be one step toward normalcy. I bought a bowl of oatmeal even though I'd already had a leftover hamburger at home—it was literally the only food in the house except expired canned peas—and headed over to our usual table with the low benches. Today, Malina was alone and the cafeteria was mostly empty. I'd kind of been hoping for others to be around as a distraction, but no such luck.

"Hey," she said, looking up from the book she was reading, which had stars and planets on the cover.

When she smiled at me, she looked totally calm and put together. She wasn't afraid to look me in the eye. It was like nothing had even happened. To her, I guessed nothing *had* happened. I just had to convince myself of that, too.

"Hey." I took the seat across from her and unwrapped my plastic spork.

"Was it nice sleeping in your own bed last night?" she asked.

I groaned. "*Yes.* The last three hotel beds I've slept in have been ridiculously uncomfortable. Plus I had to room with Matthews, who snores like a chainsaw. My bed and bedroom have never been more perfect than they were last night."

Except for the dream, I didn't add.

"That's good. You ready for your classes?"

I dove into my oatmeal. Theoretically, oatmeal was supposed to be hot, but this was the Oakview High School cafeteria. Most of the time it was lukewarm, and this made even that sound generous. "Not really. There were a few assignments I was supposed to do with my tutor that didn't get done."

She frowned and closed her book. "Why not?"

I took another bite. At least there was enough cinnamon and sugar to make up for the cold lumpiness. "You know me and school. We've never gotten along very well."

"Mmhmm," she said in her "I don't believe you" tone.

I looked up at her. "What? It's true."

"There wouldn't be a girl who's partially responsible for those incomplete assignments, would there?"

It wasn't fair that she could read me like a book when all I was doing was sitting there eating cold oatmeal. "No."

"Liar."

The teasing in her voice made me want to prove her wrong, but I couldn't. The girl knew me too well. "Fine, there was, okay? I was supposed to catch up on work, but a couple of us were hanging out in the hotel hot tub after the game, and there were these girls…" I shook my head. Coach would have lost his shit if he knew what we'd been up to after curfew.

Malina held up a hand to stop me. "Okay, that's enough information. There were girls. I got it."

"Right."

"And where are said girls now?"

I shrugged as I scraped the bottom of my bowl. "One of them added me on Snapchat." What I didn't tell Malina was the type of Snapchats they were. I definitely didn't ask for them. I wasn't that kind of guy. But apparently the girl who sent them was that kind of girl, and there was no reason to make Malina blush.

"So they left you with a Snapchat account and a pile of unfinished assignments. Sounds awesome."

Normally, I'd laugh this off or even be proud of it. Malina was just giving me a hard time, but her words still made my skin crawl. Yeah, the time with those girls had been fun. I probably wouldn't have worked on my assignments even if I hadn't been with them. School wasn't my thing, but hockey was. I could have squeezed in some weight training at the hotel gym or watched NHL games for research. Instead, I'd chosen "fun." But looking back, how much "fun" had it really been? The bad decision settled heavily in my gut. Maybe it was time for more than just fun.

"Hey," Malina said, putting her hand on my forearm.

Her touch warmed my skin and made me think way too much about my dream from last night. I yanked my arm back.

Malina startled. "Sorry. Just…where'd you go on me?"

"Sorry, sorry," I said, and tried to force an easygoing smile, which probably didn't look very easygoing. "I was thinking. About all of the homework. Maybe I'll do some of it tonight."

She frowned like she didn't believe me. Had she always been that pretty when she frowned? Wait. I shut that thought down faster than a penalty shot. If those hotel girls had been a mistake, thinking about Malina was *definitely* a mistake. For many reasons.

"Let me know if you need any help catching up," she said.

Malina was in AP and honors classes, and while I wasn't in remedial classes (yet, though a few more hotel girl nights and I might end up there next semester), I was solidly in the non-AP classes. But if I'd let her tutor me right then, all I'd think about was how much I wanted to kiss her again and how good she smelled and how I never really noticed that the shirt she'd had since freshman year fit her a whole lot differently now than it did back then…

Shit.

I stood so fast I knocked my oatmeal bowl and spork to the ground. "No," I said. "That's okay." When I bent over to pick up the trash, I smacked my head on the edge of the table on the way up.

Malina winced. "Are you okay? That sounded like it hurt."

"Fine," I said quickly. "Fine. I gotta go."

Then without waiting for a response, I hurried out of the cafeteria. When I reached my locker, I leaned back against it and closed my eyes, willing my pulse to slow back to normal.

It didn't matter what assurances she gave me when I texted her last night.

We weren't fine.

We weren't still just friends.

At least not in my book.

"Jackson!" Coach Tucker snapped. "There's no way Delecky should have made that shot! Get your head in the game or get your ass out of the goal."

"Yes, sir!" I yelled through my mask. It was the end of our afternoon practice, and he was right. I should *not* have missed that shot. As much as I wished I could say it was because I was tired or the shot was amazing, neither was true. I hadn't been paying attention. Usually I could tune out the rest of the world, including girls, when I was on the ice. That didn't seem to be possible with Malina.

I tapped the posts with my stick and blocked the next shot. I missed the one after that, but it was from the best player on our team, Pierce Miller, and there was no way I could have stopped it. Coach must have known, too, because he didn't say a word. I blocked the next two shots, but then I started wondering if Malina had told anyone about the kiss. If she'd told Izzy or her mom or Tutu. Things were already awkward enough between the two of us. The last thing I wanted was—

"Jackson!" Coach yelled as I let yet another too-easy puck into the net.

Guilt struck as quickly as that last slap shot. I swore under my breath. Letting Coach down was the worst. "Sorry."

"All right, stop," Coach yelled. "Wind sprints for the rest of practice. You can thank Jackson."

I looked down at the ice so I wouldn't have to see the entire team shooting daggers at me. They gave a collective groan, but no one talked back. We all knew better than that.

"And Jackson, if you think you're starting in goal next game after an embarrassment of a practice like that, you're wrong."

My heart sank. There had been scouts at all of our games lately. Starting in goal every game was essential, and I'd blown it. I *needed* to get my mind off Malina and on the ice. I ripped off my goalie pads and joined in with my teammates. The last ten minutes of practice had never felt so long. When Coach finally blew the whistle and told us to hit the showers, I headed back to the net on shaky legs to grab my pads. Pierce hung back just off the ice, waiting for me.

"Sorry," I said, still gasping for breath.

Pierce shrugged the apology off. "We've all earned the team wind sprints at one time or another."

He wasn't breathing nearly as hard as I was. Though I used to play left wing, I'd spent most of the last few years between the posts. My reflexes were quick—when I wasn't thinking about Malina—and being a goalie was still hard work, but my skating stamina was starting to suck. I needed to up my cardio.

"Everything okay?" Pierce asked before taking a swig from his water bottle.

He held the locker room door open for me. The room was loud and smelled like a wet dog, but I was used to it.

"Yeah," I said. A couple of the guys seemed to get that I was having a bad day and pounded me on the shoulder as I passed. A couple of other guys muttered sarcastic thanks for the wind sprints, but Pierce shut them up with a look.

"You sure?" he asked. "Seemed like your brain wasn't in it out there."

I sighed and tossed my pads in the bottom of my locker. "That obvious?"

"To those of us who were paying attention, yeah. Where *was* your brain?"

This was ridiculous. I didn't need to waste Pierce's time on a thing that wasn't even a thing. So I'd accidentally kissed my friend. There had been plenty of times I could have kissed her before, but hadn't. The majority of the girls I'd dated weren't bothered by Malina. Our friendship was obviously nothing more than that. Hell, during freshman year homecoming, my date had been fine with me dancing with Malina. That night, in the middle of the dark school gym, we'd danced to a slow song, and I hadn't kissed her then. Not when my hands were on her back on the silky fabric of her dress. Not when her heels made her the same height as freshman-me, our mouths close together. Not when I could feel her breath on my skin as she laughed and—

"*Jackson*," Miller said.

"Huh?" When I looked up, Pierce was tugging his practice jersey up over his head. Most of the other guys had already disappeared in the direction of the showers. Yet there I was, still fully clothed.

"It's about a girl, isn't it?"

It probably should have bugged me when everyone assumed that right away, but it was also true. "Yeah. Kind of."

Pierce grinned and thwacked his jersey against my arm. "I knew you couldn't stay single for long, but it's not like you to get this distracted over a girl. This one must be special. Does that mean I should learn her name?"

I looked at the ground as I spoke because he already knew her name. "Malina."

"I'm sorry, what?"

If my cheeks hadn't been flushed from the wind sprints before, they were then. "You heard me."

"Do you happen to know more than one Malina, or…?"

"Or did I kiss my best friend? Yeah. That." I unearthed the bottles of body wash and shampoo from the back of my locker.

"Okay, so you kissed Malina. That's awesome, right? Dating your best friend?"

If only it were that easy. If only. "No. We're not dating. I accidentally kissed her. And she wasn't into it, but I was, and now everything is fucked up."

A look of confusion crossed Pierce's face. "Wait, you *accidentally* kissed her? How does that happen?"

"I didn't mean to. We were just sitting on the couch like we always do, and I'd missed her so much while we were traveling, and it just happened." I took off my jersey and shoved it in the bottom of my bag.

"Okay," Pierce said, like he didn't really get it, but would go along with it for my sake. "When did this happen?"

"Last night."

"And now things are awkward between you two?"

"Very."

"Well, it's only been a day, man. Give her a chance to process. You said she wasn't into it? Maybe it caught her off guard. See what happens. Either she'll realize she actually can be into it, or…"

My hopes climbed up a notch. Was there some way to make this okay that I hadn't thought about? "…Or?"

"Or you'll live a pathetic life of celibacy while having wet dreams about your best friend who doesn't want you back."

My hopes plummeted back to the locker room floor. I punched him in the shoulder. "Shut up, man. You can only joke about that kind of thing because you already have Lia."

Pierce had this smile that he only got when his girlfriend, Lia Bailey, was involved. It was the real-life equivalent of the heart-eye emoji.

But he stuffed the smile down and gave me another look of sympathy. "Give it some time. Push past the awkward and see if things go back to normal or take a different direction. And hey, you could always invite her to Matthews' party this weekend. Just as friends or whatever. I'm bringing Lia."

That was an idea. I wasn't sure if it was a terrible or amazing idea, but I had some time to figure that out. "Yeah.

Maybe."

"Good. Okay. I'm hitting the shower before those assholes use all the hot water."

"Hey, Pierce?"

He threw a towel over one shoulder and looked back to me. "Yeah?"

"Want to do some extra conditioning this weekend? On ice or off?"

He smiled. "Nothing like wind sprints to make you feel like you're going soft between those posts, right?"

"Exactly."

"I'm in. Text me whenever."

Conditioning. Hockey. I could stay focused on those things. I *needed* to stay focused on those things. And Pierce was right. With Malina, I could just wait to see what would happen. Things were awkward because I was *making* them awkward. I just needed to make them something else.

Chapter Five

Malina

Math and science were simple. They were based on facts. Procedures. Proof. Essay writing, on the other hand, was subjective. That was why I was staring at my computer, deleting and replacing the same sentence of a college scholarship application essay over and over again.

The Melting toP was busy that night. Lots of people talking, plenty more working on computers like me, and even one guy who appeared to be taking a nap in one of the plush chairs in the corner. In short, it was the perfect place to get lost in homework, which made the café my third favorite place in the world. The first was space. The second was home—preferably on the couch with Jackson, kissing optional.

I *really* needed to stop thinking about Jackson.

I shook off the thought, literally, and tried to focus on something—anything—else. Staring at the Melting toP's sign, with its gold and blue swirls that had always reminded me of a galaxy, worked. The place hadn't always been called The

Melting toP. The *P* and *t* used to be in the right places, but when some big fondue restaurant caught wind of our town's little business, they sent a cease and desist letter requiring them to change their name. The owner took a ladder outside, switched the *P* and the *t*, and called it The Melting toP. It got the lawyers off his back and added to the café's charm.

The place had a little bit of everything. It was always a coffee shop and an ice cream store with some of the best soft serve I'd ever tasted. There was a different flavor each day, and you could add this chocolate sauce that made me want to lick my bowl. The ice cream was popular even in the dead of winter in Michigan. But the third section of The Melting toP changed based on the owner's ideas or what was popular at the time. Once it had been a cereal bar with like thirty-seven types of cereal and ten kinds of milk. Another time, it was a make-your-own-grilled-cheese bar, with more fillings than could possibly fit between two pieces of bread. A couple of summers ago, it was a s'mores bar, and the place almost burned down. Currently, it was a pancake bar, which made the whole place smell sweet, like syrup.

Sufficiently distracted, I turned my attention back to my essay. Then I decided I didn't like the last three words I'd written, so I deleted them, along with the three before that for good measure. I was giving an "I'm never going to finish this essay" sigh when I saw Jackson sit down at a table a few feet away from mine, a giant bowl of soft serve in his hands. I hadn't even seen him come in.

"Jackson," I said.

When he looked up, his eyes went wide, like he wasn't expecting to see me there. For a second, he hesitated. The slightly panicked look on his face as he walked over was definitely the look of someone who regretted a kiss. Jackson being unhappy to see me was a new low. It stung, but I gritted my teeth against the quick, sharp pain and forced a smile.

Pretend it didn't happen. "Hey."

"Hey." He nodded toward my computer. "Busy?"

I glanced at the clock in the corner of my screen. I'd discovered this particular scholarship late in the game, and applications were due in a few hours. "Kind of. This scholarship essay is due soon, but my brain and fingers aren't cooperating."

"Maybe a break would help?" Without waiting for my response, he sat down across from me and shoveled a big bite of ice cream into his mouth.

A bite so big I knew exactly what was going to happen. "Probably," I said, and waited. Three...two...

Jackson dropped his spoon and put one hand to his head. "Ah! Brain freeze."

I waited for his hand to drop, then asked, "Better?"

"Yeah. Why didn't you stop me from taking a bite that big?"

"Because the one time I did that, you tried to bite my hand."

"Oh yeah." He grinned that one-white-tooth grin. "Sorry. I must have been hungry."

Okay, grinning was good. We could do this. We could have a normal conversation like before The-Event-That-Must-Not-Be-Named. I nodded toward his bowl. "What flavor is it today?"

"Cherry." He took a less brain-freeze-inducing bite. "Really good with the chocolate sauce. Man, I missed this place. Want some?"

I shook my head and took a sip from my chai tea latte. It was too delicious to ruin with ice cream. "No, thanks." Jackson's hair was damp, and even over all the syrup, I could smell the shampoo and body wash he used at the rink. It smelled clean and a little bit spicy, not like the overly-strong stuff most of our classmates used. But since when was the way

Jackson smelled so distracting? "How was practice?"

"Not great. I sucked, and then Coach made the whole team do wind sprints because of it. I'm out of shape."

I couldn't resist a jab. "Couldn't have anything to do with those giant bowls of ice cream you eat, could it?"

He pointed his spoon at me. "I'll have you know that I burned off every single one of these calories today. Probably even more than that." Then he took a "take that" bite to prove it.

"You know I'm teasing," I said.

Silence settled over us. Usually, there weren't many silences between us, and those that happened were comfortable, but this was decidedly uncomfortable. He took another bite. I took another drink. Ugh, what *was* this? I didn't know how to do this. Not with Jackson.

"So," I said.

At the very same time he said, "Hey."

Was it my imagination, or did his cheeks turn a little pink? Probably it was leftover pink from the wind sprints.

"Go ahead," I said.

"How are the college applications going?"

Thankfully, this was something I could talk about. "Good. I've applied to Western, Central, Grand Valley, and Saginaw Valley. Now I'm working on some scholarship applications so I'll actually be able to afford one of those if I do get accepted."

"*When* you get accepted." But then he frowned. "What about the rest?"

"What do you mean?"

"What about Caltech and Williams College and Harvard and Princeton? What about all those schools you researched with the really good astrophysics programs?"

I toyed with the cardboard Melting toP sleeve on my latte cup. "I researched those back when I was a freshman. Back when I was dreaming. Before I knew better."

"Knew better than what?"

"Before I knew about things like out-of-state tuition, for example. I wouldn't be able to get enough scholarships to cover it. My parents haven't saved that much money. I can't put that on them. And speaking of my parents, I'll major in business and I'll walk out of graduation with a job. I already have an 'in' at my dad's company. It's steady. Stable. You know the story. My dad majored in sociology, which was interesting, but didn't lead to a career. He had to start at the bottom and work ridiculously hard the whole way up. He's doing his best to give me a better start than he had."

Jackson dropped his spoon and let his chin fall to his chest with his eyes closed, letting out an exaggerated fake snore that made a few people at nearby tables glance over at him.

My cheeks warmed. "*Jackson*."

His head snapped back up, and he opened his eyes. "What? Sorry. I fell asleep for a second. What completely boring thing were you talking about? Oh, wait. On second thought, tell me something about astrophysics."

I frowned. "What?"

"Tell me something astrophysics-y. Anything."

That was an odd request. Sure, Jackson endured my scientific blathering every once in a while, but he definitely never *requested* it. I wasn't about to let an opportunity to talk to someone—anyone—about it go, though. "So I read this article last week about a new way to measure the mass and radius of a star. Before, it would take years and thousands of measurements to figure that out, which is still incredible, but now—"

"There," he said, without waiting for me to finish my sentence.

I blinked at him. "What?"

"That's the look. You get this look on your face when you're talking about space or science or whatever. Like you're thinking incredibly hard but so ridiculously happy about it."

He pressed one thumb to my cheek. It was cold from his ice cream bowl. The touch was innocent and quick, but the feel of his skin against mine lingered after he removed his hand.

"You turn this adorable shade of pink. You geek out and love every second of it. That's what you should study in college. That's what you should do for a living. Something you love that much."

Even though I'd just been talking about a highly technical process, every single word had gone missing from my brain. Whatever pink was in my cheeks right then couldn't be blamed solely on talking about something science-related anymore. What was *up* with me? No. No, no, no. This couldn't happen. We were friends. Jackson was bound to touch me. We shared platonic hugs and fist bumps and playful nudges all the time. I hadn't ever turned to mush because of those touches before, and I couldn't start then.

I cleared my throat. "So does that mean you should study that bowl of ice cream in college? You look like you're pretty in love with that, too."

"If majoring in ice cream was a thing, I'd graduate with honors. Probably get my master's in it." He laughed and took another bite. "Maybe even a PhD."

I chuckled, both knowing he was right and enjoying the fact that I'd successfully distracted him from talking about me and me from having a complete non-friend-like meltdown. "You're lucky you'll be chosen by a team instead of choosing a university."

"NHL or bust. And there won't be a bust."

The thought of Jackson possibly having to move to another state to play for a team made my smile disappear. I really wanted Jackson to accomplish his dreams and be happy. Two days ago, I would have said the separation we had the past year or so while he focused on hockey and I focused on school was natural preparation for that. The kiss might have changed how I felt, but it hadn't changed our situation.

"And they'll be lucky to have you," I said.

"Thanks." He scraped the last bite of ice cream out of his bowl. "Hey, Malina?"

"Yeah?"

He hesitated a second too long. "What are you doing this weekend?"

I grabbed my phone and checked out my calendar, which was pretty full. "I'm volunteering twice, trying to get more hours in. Plus, I have a few tests next week and a scholarship application due, so most of my time will be spent on that."

He nodded. "Oh, yeah. Right."

"Why?" I asked. "What are you up to?"

"Nothing," he said quickly. Too quickly. "I mean, lots of things. No game, but practices and work outs, and I convinced Miller to do some extra training with me."

That was weird. Why had he asked about my weekend when he was busy with hockey? This post-kiss awkwardness needed to go away. And fast.

I swallowed the last sip of my chai, which was cold but still sweet. Since it was obvious I wasn't going to get work done, I closed my laptop. "I should probably go home and work on this since I can't seem to concentrate here." Meaning, I needed some distance from *Jackson*.

He nodded. "I should probably go home and see if my mom went grocery shopping. I grabbed food with a couple of the guys, but I'm feeling a second dinner night."

Despite the awkwardness, I couldn't help but smile as we packed up our stuff. "You know, for some people, one dinner plus a giant serving of ice cream is more than enough."

He nodded toward the pancake bar as we walked toward the exit. "Hey, be proud that I'm not grabbing pancakes on the way out. Maybe second dinner will include vegetables."

I laughed and shivered as we walked into the dark, cold night. I took my mom's car keys out of my pocket. "See you tomorrow?"

"No. Teacher work day, remember?"

What was that cringe-worthy feeling somewhere near my stomach? Was it really disappointment over not seeing Jackson? Even after this mostly awkward interaction? I needed to get a grip. Immediately. "Oh, yeah. I forgot."

"Coach somehow found out and scheduled extra practice for those of us who have the day off."

"That was nice of him."

"So nice."

We stood there, staring at each other. He seemed to be looking for something in my expression, and the intensity there freaked me out a little. Once again, heat crept into my cheeks. If we were dating—which we were *not*—I imagined this was when he'd kiss me good night.

Why, oh why did I suddenly like the idea?

Nope. Not going down that rabbit hole. I tried to focus on reality. On the fact that my best friend wasn't acting like my best friend anymore. Before the other night, he'd have at least hugged me. That didn't seem to be an option anymore.

"Well, have fun," I said awkwardly, "and I guess I'll see you when I see you?"

"Yeah. See you," Jackson echoed.

I tried to ignore how swoony I felt when he watched me walk away.

At home, my concentration on essays wasn't any better. Every time I tried to focus, my mind drifted to Jackson. Which sent me straight back to the kiss. He wasn't the first guy to kiss me. I'd had the same boyfriend all of freshman year, until he cheated on me with some girl he met at summer camp. While I was with that guy, the kissing was fine. It was good. But it wasn't great. That kiss with Jackson? It was *great*. Did it shock me? Yes. Did I freak out after? Yes. But it made me feel like all those kisses with my first boyfriend were the equivalent of kissing a warm piece of bologna.

At this rate of distraction, I was going to have a maximum of two and a half sentences to turn in when this essay was due at midnight. Fantastic. I picked up my phone and opened my messages to Izzy. If there was one person I could count on to get my mind off a guy, it was her, mostly because she had never been and would never be interested in guys. Maybe some girls would miss having a straight friend they could drool over guys with, but I wouldn't trade my best friend for the world. I thumbed out a new message to her.

Me: *What are you up to?*

Izzy: *Working on a scholarship application. I think this one wants a blood sample, a full-length novel, and two of my eyelashes.*

I smiled when I read her response. Unlike Jackson, Izzy also understood the need for and importance of scholarships. She was big into fashion, and was incredibly talented with her designs, but design schools weren't cheap.

Me: *Same here. No eyelash requests yet, though. Want to come work here? Mine is due tonight, and I need help focusing.*

Izzy: *Yes please! Be right over.*

I set the phone down and turned back to the computer. This particular application had a choice of writing prompts to respond to. Originally, I'd chosen the "what makes you different" prompt and planned to talk about my Hawaiian heritage. But so far, I only had five words: Hawaii is a beautiful place.

Sigh. I hit delete and scrolled through the other essay choices. While I was scrolling, there was a knock on the door. Izzy lived on the next street over, which made hanging out easy since neither of us had our own car.

"It's Izzy," I called as I got up. My parents and Tutu were in the living room, watching some police drama they watched every single week.

By the time I got to the front door, my dad had already opened it.

"Hey, Izzy. Lovely hair, as always."

My family hadn't seen Izzy since she'd done her hair last weekend. Her natural color was blonde to the point of almost being white, which made it the perfect palette for whatever color she wanted to throw at it. Currently, there were wide sections that started blue up near the roots, and melted into purple and pink toward the tips. The girl would also do really well in cosmetology school if she wanted. She'd tried to dye my hair before, but since I had my mom's Hawaiian black hair, it didn't show up. She said I'd have to completely bleach it first, which I wasn't willing to do.

"Thanks, Mr. Hall," Izzy said. "Hey, Mrs. Hall. Hi, Tutu. Oh, is that *Under Arrest*? I just watched last week's episode with the—"

"The cop who ended up being one of the criminals?" Mom asked. "Yes! That one was so good, and this one's even better!"

My dad returned to his seat, and the four of them stared at the screen, where a "cop" who was far too gorgeous to be a cop in real life was digging through some evidence.

I let Izzy watch for a second, then cleared my throat

loudly. She didn't look my way, or at least she didn't until I kicked her leg.

"Ow! What?"

I looked meaningfully toward the kitchen.

"Oh. Right. Scholarships."

Izzy sat in the seat next to me and opened her computer. The laptop was covered with stickers she'd collected over the past few years. There was even a little Hawaiian flag sticker I'd brought back for her when we took a trip to visit Mom's family, before Tutu came to live with us.

"I swear, with how much work is required for some of these scholarships and the little amount of money that's available, we're earning like four dollars an hour. I did the math. Not even minimum wage. And that's only if you actually *get* the scholarship, which isn't very likely in most cases."

"You do realize that while you were doing that math, you could have been applying for another scholarship, right?"

She waved my comment off. "What are you working on?"

"An essay. Can't find a topic I like."

"Are there any you can recycle from a different application?"

"Not really. They're mostly weird topics."

Before Izzy could respond, my phone vibrated on the table. A Snapchat from Jackson. My pulse picked up speed. Exactly what I didn't need to help my concentration. I put the phone back to sleep without looking at what he'd sent, but I wasn't quick enough for Izzy.

"Was that from Jackson? Hey, did I see him in the hall today? Is he back in town?"

Yeah, not going there. "Yep." I pointed at my screen. "Oh, maybe I'll write about this one. Where I see myself in ten years. I haven't done one of those yet, but it can't be that hard, right? I know exactly where I'll be."

But Izzy didn't take the bait. "Whoa, whoa, subject

changer. What's going on? What's up with that?"

"With what?" Even though I was playing dumb, my cheeks felt like they were on fire. Though the pigment in my skin usually hid a little blush, this wasn't a little blush.

I was screwed.

"Spill, Blushy McBlusherson. What's up with Jackson?"

"Nothing," I said, entirely too quickly. "Nothing. He's home."

"...And?"

"That's all."

"Oh my gosh, you had sex with him."

I didn't think it was possible for my cheeks to get any warmer, but they did. "No! We did not have sex." I lowered my voice and prayed my family hadn't heard any of that. "Don't be ridiculous."

"Fine, you didn't have sex. But you kissed him."

"No," I said, but couldn't look her in the eye when I said it. It wasn't *completely* true.

"Okay, I got it, I got it. *He* kissed *you*."

As much as wanted to, I couldn't disagree. I couldn't lie to my friend. "Yeah. But it was an accident."

"An accident? What the heck kind of accident ends with his lips on yours?" Izzy shoved her laptop out of the way and snatched my phone before I could stop her. And of course she knew my passcode.

"Iz," I said, but didn't really make an effort to stop her. Maybe I needed to talk about this. Maybe I needed to get it out in the open, and then I'd be able to focus like normal.

"Oh. It's something he sent to everyone. Some hockey thing." There wasn't anyone in the world who cared about sports less than Izzy.

"Oh," I said.

She frowned at me. "Malina Hall, is that disappointment I hear in your voice?" She set the phone down, folded her hands on the table, and leaned onto her forearms, looking more serious than anyone with blue, purple, and pink hair had any right to. "Start from the beginning. Tell me everything."

So I did. I told her about Jackson coming home and being at my house and how everything was so normal until it was very definitely not normal and things had been weird ever since.

When I finished, I took a long breath because that was something I'd apparently forgotten to do.

"Do you want to get in his pants?"

Seriously. Was it possible to give yourself a fever from embarrassment? Because all the blood rushing to my face made me feel way too hot. "What? No. He's my *friend*. Practically my brother. Are you insane?"

She held up her hands in an "I'm innocent" kind of way. "Okay, okay. Had to make sure. But since you don't, that makes things easier. He's your friend. Keep being his friend. Keep talking to him like normal. Nothing has to change."

She made it sound so easy… "But things *have* changed. He's being weird." I didn't mention that I'd changed and was being weird, too.

"Well, that's his problem. Not yours." Izzy ran a hand through her hair, exposing more of the blue than had been showing a second ago. "He'll get over it."

Mentally, I let myself flip that statement and think that *I'd* get over it. "You think we'll be okay?"

"I think you and Jackson will be fine. Now, you and that scholarship, on the other hand…"

"Right, right," I said. "Back to work. But let me see that."

I unlocked my phone and replayed the snap. It was a short clip of the exterior of the local ice arena, with Jackson saying how good it was to be home. How much he missed that rink.

"Are you responding? If you are, tell him I said he better not accidentally kiss me. My next kiss goes to my new girl, not some guy." She shuddered, as if completely revolted by the thought.

I rolled my eyes.

But I didn't respond. I closed out of the app, put my phone face down on the table, and got back to work. I'd given up on the possibility that this essay was going to be good, but at least I could make sure it was complete. Izzy was right. Jackson and I would be completely fine.

Chapter Six

JACKSON

When I got home from The Melting toP, I made sure I dropped my hockey bag in the laundry room and not some other random place. Mom had a pretty strict "no hockey equipment beyond the washing machine until it's clean" rule. I didn't think my gear smelled *that* bad, but she didn't seem to agree. I'd used the last of my clean practice jerseys today, so I started a load before heading into the living room.

Mom was on the couch with her phone, so I sat next to her. The leather always felt extra cold in the fall and winter, but it didn't bother me. I put my feet up on the table in front of me, already feeling the tightness in my quads and hamstrings from those wind sprints.

"Hey," I said.

"Hi, sweetie." She leaned over and kissed my cheek. "How was practice?"

"Fine," I said. I didn't really want to talk about the missed shots or the fact that I wouldn't be starting the next game.

"How was work?"

Mom was an event planner, so she tended to work weird hours. I never knew when she was going to be home or at an event, but the flexibility had been great both when I was a kid and when I started getting really into hockey and needed rides to the rink all the time.

"It was good. Working on a few holiday parties, but those are easy."

"Nice." The fall and winter were always quieter than spring and summer, which were full of graduation parties and weddings. "Did you happen to go grocery shopping?"

She took a sip of wine from her glass on the end table. "I picked up a few things." She glanced at the clock. "Why? I thought you said you were eating with the guys?"

"I did," I said. "But I'm still hungry."

She sighed. "When you're gone, I always forget that you eat me out of house and home. But come on, you can't possibly tell me you didn't stop at The Melting Pot, too. You've only mentioned how much you missed it twenty times in the past week."

"It's The Melting *toP*. And it wasn't twenty times. Probably only nineteen."

"Mmhmm." She toyed with a loose thread on the sweater she was wearing. "And what flavor ice cream did they have today?"

"Cherry."

"Yum. Well, I'm not enabling your second-dinner habit. If you want something, you can make it yourself."

I put a hand over my heart like I was wounded. "Ouch. And the Mother of the Year award goes to…"

She rolled her eyes and turned back to her phone. Actually, the couch was pretty comfortable. Maybe I was more tired than hungry. It was then that I noticed something on Mom's phone. There were pictures on the screen, and she was studying each one for a few seconds before swiping left or right.

"Wait," I said. "What are you doing?"

Mom glanced up before turning her phone away from my view. "None of your business."

I leaned over so I could see again. "Are you on Tinder?"

"Honey, we talked about this. You know I've been doing some online dating."

My parents had divorced a few years ago. It had happened out of the blue. It wasn't like they'd been fighting for years, or if they had been, they'd hid it well. But they didn't fight much during the divorce either, not even over who I would live with or how much time I would spend with each parent, so it wasn't terrible for me. My dad only lived about twenty minutes away.

"Yeah, but I thought you were on Seniors Dating Seniors or something like that," I said.

"Hey," Mom said. "Watch your mouth."

I leaned over farther to get a better look at her screen. "Are there seriously old people on Tinder?"

"I am *not* old!"

Okay, maybe my mom wasn't *that* old, but the guy on the screen definitely was. The picture was a shirtless mirror selfie, complete with flabby arms, a bald head, and a pudgy waist. He wasn't even smiling.

"No," I said. "No, no, no. Get away from that."

I tried to take the phone from her, but she held it out of my reach.

"Luke! Stop! I'm a grown woman and can do what I want."

Switching tactics, I pulled my phone out of my pocket and tapped the screen a few times.

"What's that noise? What are you doing? Are you FaceTiming someone?"

Before Mom could say anything else, the phone connected and my sister's face appeared on my screen.

"Lukey! Hey stranger! What's up?"

Lacey was the only human being in the world I tolerated

calling me that. She was a junior in college on the other side of the state. Currently, her hair was pulled back in a messy bun and there was a pen tucked behind her ear, like I'd caught her studying. I could tell from the poster on the wall behind her that she was in her bedroom in her apartment.

"Please tell Mom that she cannot be on Tinder."

"Hey!" Mom said. "No fair ganging up on me!"

"Mom, you're on *Tinder*?" Lacey asked. "What? Why?"

"You know the guys your age on there have to be creeps, right?" I asked. "Lace, back me up on this."

"Hand me to her," Lacey said.

I obliged, and Mom gave a dramatic sigh before setting her own phone down and taking mine.

"Hey, Lace," she said, like we weren't in the middle of a conversation. "How's school?"

"It's fine. Stay on topic. This is a terrible idea. Half the guys on there are married, and the other half are on the sex offenders list."

Mom scoffed. "That's not true. I'm on there, and neither of those things is true about me!"

I snatched back both my phone and Mom's. I flipped the camera on my phone around so Lacey could see the guy on the screen. "Look at this," I said. "There's no way this guy is married, so he's got to be a sex offender."

"Oh my gosh, Mom!" Lacey cried. "Swipe left! Swipe left!"

"You two, so quick to judge based on looks," Mom said, shaking her head.

"Uh, that's exactly what Tinder *is*," I pointed out.

"Fine," Mom said, and took her phone back so she could swipe left.

Only the next guy was even worse. It was another mirror selfie. Thankfully this one was fully clothed, but he was also visibly holding his junk.

"Oh my gosh!" Mom said. "What is that man doing? Why

would he make that his picture?"

On my phone, Lacey started cracking up. "Left, Mom. Left."

Instead of swiping left, Mom swiped out of the app completely. "I swear, the first couple of guys I saw seemed completely normal."

"Can't you stick to meeting guys at the library or something?" I asked.

Mom quirked an eyebrow at me. "When was the last time you were at the library?"

Lacey sighed. "Online dating is fine, but maybe stick to a different site?"

"Fine, fine. If you two insist."

"Good. Hey, let me talk to Luke, okay? I want to hear how hockey's going."

"Okay. Love you, hon. I'll talk to you later," Mom said.

I headed upstairs with my phone. "Thank you. Seriously. I didn't think she was going to listen to me, and that...can't happen."

"Absolutely," she said. "Glad I could help."

"So how's school?"

"Meh. Hard. Boring. Exhausting. Maybe I don't want to do this 'lawyer' thing anymore."

I laughed. Lacey had learned to argue before I was born and never looked back. Though there weren't any lawyers in our family, it was still practically in her DNA. "Yeah right. Been to any good parties lately?"

"There are no parties in college," she said, completely straight faced. "That's a bunch of rumors you see on TV and in movies."

I rolled my eyes. "You don't have to lie to me. I'm not going to college. Even if I were, that lie wouldn't be enough to convince me."

"Damn," she said. "I'll have to work on that. How's hockey?"

"Good. I'm home for a couple of weeks." I didn't tell

her about practice today. I couldn't tell her why I'd been so distracted. Couldn't admit to her that I'd kissed Malina. Like most people, Lacey had given me a hard time about Malina when we first started hanging out, thinking I'd liked her, but when a year or two passed with us just as friends, she gave up.

"What are you thinking about?" Lacey asked.

Oh, crap. I'd been staring blankly at a wall. I snapped my attention back to the screen. "What? Nothing. Sorry."

She quirked one eyebrow in a classic Lacey gesture. "I'm not buying that. Spill."

"It's nothing," I said.

"It's a girl," she said.

Why did *everyone* automatically go there? Was it written all over my face? "What's that? You're breaking up. Our connection must be bad. I gotta go."

Lacey laughed. "Fine. Don't tell me, asshole. I gotta get back to studying. Feel free to FaceTime me sometime when you *don't* need something, okay?"

"Deal."

"Love you, Lukey."

"Love you, too."

I ended the connection. Even though I was tired and wanted nothing more than to collapse onto my bed, I needed to do my weight lifting for the day. Thankfully, it was an arm day, so Coach's wind sprints wouldn't affect me. I changed into sweats and headed down to the basement, where I had a small gym set up.

I turned up the music loud enough to distract me from thinking about old people on Tinder or bad hockey practices. Even then, it wasn't loud enough to keep thoughts of Malina from slipping through. I was in deep and had no idea how to dig myself out.

Chapter Seven

MALINA

"*Aloha kakahiaka*," I said, placing a kiss on the top of Tutu's head. The conditioner she used smelled like honey.

"*Aloha 'auinalā*," she said.

There was a slight smile on her face and teasing tone to her voice as she responded "good afternoon" to my "good morning." I glanced at the clock. It wasn't afternoon, but it was pretty close. I'd worked on that scholarship essay and application until the last possible second, submitting at 11:59. Thanks to my distraction, it was far from my best work. I'd felt so guilty about submitting something subpar that I couldn't sleep, and ended up tinkering with my planet project for another hour or two, which was almost as unsuccessful as the scholarship application.

I took a seat next to Tutu at the kitchen table. A box that had arrived from Hawaii was open on the floor, and several cylinders of tightly wrapped dried leaves tied with yarn sat on the table. Tutu had opened one of the cylinders, so a pile of loose, curly dried leaves was also on the table.

"*Kuka'a*?" I asked, touching one of the still-wrapped cylinders of *lauhala*.

Tutu smiled at me, wrinkles deepening around her eyes. "*Kuka'a*," she said, correcting my pronunciation of the term ever so slightly.

I nodded toward the knife and leaf in her hands. "What are you doing?"

Instead of responding, she held the knife to one end of the long, dry leaf and pulled in a quick, confident tug. She was left with two long pieces—one thicker and darker, but smaller than the other. She held that piece up. "The bone. It's not used in weaving." She placed it on the floor, where "bones" were accumulating in a pile. Then she held up the other. "The *lau* is used in weaving."

I held up one of the whole leaves. The difference between the bone and the *lau* was obvious. "Can I try?" I always wanted to learn anything I could from Tutu.

She smiled and handed over the knife. She made a slight tear at the top of the leaf and adjusted the knife in my hand. I'd been holding it like I was going to cut a piece of steak, but she turned it more like I was going to curl a piece of ribbon. "Go," she said.

I tried to mimic the move I'd seen her do, to slide the knife like butter down the leaf, but something went wrong, and I ended up cutting through the leaf instead. "Oops."

Tutu flipped the leaf over so I was holding the other end. She made the same tear and lined the knife up for me, adjusting the leaf in my left hand. Her hand shook slightly. It was a constant reminder of the stroke she'd had a couple of years ago, but clearly it didn't hold her back too much.

"Keep it straight," she said.

I focused on holding the knife straight, and managed to remove the bone, if a little slower and sloppier than Tutu.

"Good," she said, adding the bone to her pile and handing me another leaf. "Again."

This time, I made the tear and lined up the knife. When I pulled the knife down, it felt more natural. It would take me a while to get up to Tutu's speed, but it was a start.

Tutu patted my hand and got up from the creaky old chair. She walked over to a drawer near the kitchen sink, and when she returned, she held another knife. She sat, and we started working with the *lauhala* side by side.

"What are you going to make?" I asked.

There were various woven items throughout our house—beautiful baskets and placemats and trivets—some from when Mom and Dad were in Hawaii, some mailed to us from Tutu when I was little, a few made by Tutu since she'd been living with us. Her friends mailed her rolls of leaves, or *Kuka'a*, so she could make whatever she wanted.

"We'll see," Tutu said with a shrug. The few times I'd been able to watch her weave, it almost seemed like she didn't know what the leaves were going to be until she started working with them. It was such a foreign concept to someone like me, who always knew exactly where I was going and how to get there.

We worked quietly side by side, the piles of *lau* bones building at our feet.

"You were up late last night," Tutu said.

I frowned. I'd been listening to music, but I thought I'd kept it quiet. "Did I wake you? I'm sorry."

Tutu waved off my apology before reaching for another leaf. "I saw the light."

I knew Tutu had trouble sleeping. Whether it was another side effect of the stroke or from getting older was up in the air, but I'd gotten used to hearing her making tea at odd hours of the night.

"I was working on a scholarship application and my

project." The particular leaf I'd grabbed was a little thicker and tougher than the rest, so I concentrated on it while I talked. "I stayed up too late, but I wasn't tired."

Tutu cupped one hand around my cheek. "You work too hard," she said.

I smiled. "I like working hard." I nodded toward the pile of leaves. "Just like you."

With that, she smiled back and returned to the *lauhala*. My phone buzzed in the pocket of my jeans. I removed it and saw Jackson's name on the screen. The butterflies that appeared in my stomach every time I thought about him could fly away anytime now.

Jackson: *Are you home?*

That was odd. I thought he was supposed to be at a daytime practice for the NTDP players who didn't have school. Heaven forbid they get a day off. I set my knife down and thumbed out a response.

Me: *Yes. Why?*

While waiting for another message, there was a knock at the front door.

"I'll get it," I said. I headed over and peeked through the curtain covering the tall, narrow window next to the door. I froze. Even my heart froze, skipping a beat or two or seven before pounding frantically against my ribs, trying to make up for lost time. What was Jackson doing there? I tried to stay calm and collected as I opened the door. "Hey."

"Hey," he said.

Or at least that's what I *thought* he said. His voice was hoarse and thick, like he had a cold. I motioned him inside and closed the door against the cold outside. "What's wrong? Are you okay? Aren't you supposed to be at practice right now?"

He just looked at me and sniffled. "I don't know which one of those questions you want me to answer," he said. Then he coughed and walked over to the couch, where he flopped down face first.

I sat down on the edge of the coffee table. My six-foot-tall, manly hockey player of a friend was quite a sight—feet sticking off the end of the couch, nose and cheeks red either from the temperature cold or the illness cold, huddling into his coat like it was the last warmth on Earth, fists tucked up under his chin like a kid. I tried my questions again, one at a time. "Are you okay?"

"No," he said, but the *n* sounded more like a *d*. "I'm dying."

This was typical Jackson. I remembered once during our freshman year when he broke his arm playing hockey. He kept playing for the rest of the period, until his coach realized how bad it was and made him sit the bench before going to get x-rays, which resulted in a cast from his fingers to his elbow. But give that same guy a cold, and all of the toughness went out the window.

I pushed the awkwardness of the past two days aside. None of that mattered if Jackson was sick. I untied his shoes and slipped them off his feet. He curled up on his side, tucking his feet against the end of the couch. "Too sick to be at practice?"

"Yeah. I tried to go, but I kept coughing. Coach sent me home." As if to demonstrate this fact, he coughed.

I leaned back a little bit. If he got me sick, he was going to be in trouble. At least I didn't have to worry about wanting to kiss him, but I did feel bad. He sounded miserable. "So why aren't you at home in bed?"

He gave a one-shouldered shrug that rustled his coat. "My mom is working some event all day. I didn't want to be alone." He coughed again, this time so hard his eyes watered.

This brought Tutu into the living room, *lauhala* and knife still in her hands. "Jackson?" she asked with a frown.

He looked up at her and smiled, which would have been adorable if he didn't follow it up by sneezing so hard it almost gave *me* a headache. Poor guy.

"Hey, Tutu."

She said something in Hawaiian, too fast and advanced for me to understand, but the tone made it clear she was unhappy with Jackson's current state of wellness. "You're sick," she said. "You need *mamaki*. And soup." She nodded at me, in full-on Tutu mode. "Get him a blanket and a pillow." Then she disappeared into the kitchen.

"Are you *sure* you don't want to be at home alone?" I asked.

He smiled and sneezed twice. "I love Tutu. But what is *mamki*?"

"*Mamaki*," I corrected, and wrinkled my nose. "Hawaiian medicinal tea. I'll tell her to put lots of honey and lemon in it. Be right back." I ran up the stairs to my bedroom and grabbed a pillow and blanket. Then I stopped by the bathroom to grab a box of tissues. For a second, I let myself wonder. What was Jackson really doing there? He wasn't sick enough that he *couldn't* be alone. If he told his mom he was too sick to be at practice, she'd probably leave work to take care of him anyway. And our couch wasn't as comfortable as his bed. Yet there he was.

When I got back downstairs, Jackson hadn't moved an inch. His eyes were closed, but I could tell he wasn't sleeping. The boy could—and did—sleep anywhere at any time even when healthy, so he must not have been very comfortable in order to still be awake.

"Here," I said.

When he opened his eyes, he sat up a little so I could put

the pillow down on the end of the couch. He took off his coat and settled back against the pillow, adjusting a few times. After I covered him with a blanket, he said, "Thank you." Only it sounded more like "thadk you."

I sat down on the edge of the coffee table again. Now he looked ready to sleep, but I needed to keep him awake until Tutu could get some tea into him. "Must be killing you for practice to be going on without you."

He nodded and sniffled. "First practice I've ever missed. But it was really cold. And I kept having to stop because I was sneezing or coughing. I was too tired to really skate, but my last practice was rough, and I really wanted to show Coach that I'm not losing my touch…"

I patted his arm. "You'll show him that as soon as you're feeling better. Or, if I know you as well as I think I do, you'll show him before you're completely better, as soon as you're able to be upright and make it around the rink without sneezing."

"You know me pretty well."

At that moment, Tutu entered the living room, carrying a steaming mug. Jackson sat up against the pillow, and she handed it over to him.

"*Mamaki*," she said. "It's Hawaiian leaves that are used to make tea for wellness."

"Did you put lots of honey and lemon in it?" I asked. Once, when I had strep throat, I'd been victim of *mamaki* without honey and lemon, and it was an experience from which I wanted to shield Jackson.

"Yes, of course," Tutu said. "Drink. It will make you better."

Jackson took a tentative sip. Tutu waited patiently. "It's good," he said after a few seconds. "Hot, but good. Thank you, Tutu."

Tutu beamed. "I'm making you soup. You'll be well in no

time." Then she shuffled back to the kitchen.

So much for my *lauhala* lesson. I saw where I rated in comparison to Jackson.

"My mom didn't have any soup in the pantry." Jackson rubbed at one of his red-rimmed eyes. "What kind of parent doesn't keep soup on hand in case her kid gets sick?"

With a lurch in my stomach, it clicked into place: the real reason why Jackson was there. It had nothing to do with me. I forced a smile. "Ah, so you're using me for my grandma and our pantry, huh?"

He went wide eyed. "No. Of course not. I wanted—"

"I'm kidding," I said, even though I hadn't been. Not completely. "You're sick. You deserve to be in a place where people will take care of you and make you sick-people food. Speaking of"—I lowered my voice a little—"how's the tea, really? I won't tell Tutu. Do you need more honey?"

"Honestly, it's good. Feels good on my throat."

"Good." I nodded toward the TV. "Want to watch a movie or an episode of *The Haunting*?"

"Sure," he said after taking another sip.

I grabbed the remote, and he shifted a little so I could sit next to him. "I get to pick because you'll be asleep before the opening credits are over."

"Never," he said.

"Always."

Sure enough, I picked a movie, Jackson finished his tea, and before the last of the opening credits, he fell asleep with his head on my shoulder, coughing a little less and breathing a little easier than he had been before the tea.

That's all he wanted. Tea. Tutu. To have a shoulder to sleep on. Any shoulder. It had nothing to do with me.

And I tried to tell myself that was okay.

But I also didn't move an inch.

Chapter Eight

JACKSON

"Why aren't you working on your project?" I asked and then sniffled. We'd watched a few movies—or, rather, *Malina* had watched a few movies while I slept—but we were just sitting in the dark while she scrolled through her phone and I finished the soup Tutu had made me. I couldn't taste much of anything, but even just the warmth of the soup helped. I couldn't remember the last time I had been this sick. Even worse than the coughing or headache or sore throat was just how *gross* I felt.

"Because I'm sitting here taking care of you," Malina said, but her tone was teasing.

Could I have taken care of myself? Sure. Did I want to? No. And I felt sorry enough for myself in my weakened state that I gave in and let myself spend the day at her house.

"Will you work on it if I leave?" I asked, setting my empty bowl on the coffee table.

"Maybe. But you don't have to leave if you don't want to."

"Thanks, but I should go." As much as I didn't want to go, my mom was home from work, and I was feeling the "going to pass out for the entire night" kind of tired. This day had been an exception. As soon as I went home and got better, I'd be back to focusing on hockey. She'd be back to focusing on school. I'd also be back to trying to forget about the kiss, but that didn't mean I was happy about it. What Pierce had said the other day ran through my mind. Maybe there was one way to make this day less of an exception. Or maybe it was my head cold dulling my senses, but I asked, "Hey, do you want to come to a party with me?"

"A party?" she asked. "With you? Now?"

"No. Friday. But yeah. A team party. Matthews said we could bring a friend or whoever. Just celebrating the fact that we're in town and have a night off."

Both the fact that she didn't say anything and the hesitant look on her face let me know this had been a terrible idea. Of course she didn't want to go to a party with me.

"I don't know," she said. "I really do have a lot of homework and volunteering to do this weekend. I'm not sure—"

Before she could finish her sentence, I sneezed five times, waited to see if there was going to be a sixth, and then groaned.

She handed me the box of tissues and said, "But I don't know that I can turn down a dying man's last wish."

For a second, I had no clue what she was talking about. It was like my brain was an Etch A Sketch and sneezing had wiped my thoughts clean. But then I remembered. "You mean you'll go to the party?"

"Maybe," she said. "If I get enough work done. And if you're less of a biohazard by then."

The tight disappointment I'd been prepared for was replaced with hope. "I will be," I said, and cleared my throat to fight back a cough that would negate that statement. "It'll be fun. You deserve a night off. But for now" — I stood, hesitating for a second when my stuffy head made me dizzy — "I should let you work on your project. Maybe tonight's the night you figure it out."

"Yeah. Maybe your germs have magical STEM properties and they've spread all over me."

I sniffled. "Sorry."

She laughed. "Kidding. You're fine."

This would usually be when I'd hug her. I'd hugged her a thousand times after nights of hanging out like this. Normally, I'd want to hug her to thank her for taking care of me and to steal a tiny bit more comfort from her before heading home. But would I be able to hug her without kissing her? Wondering that felt crazy, but then again, the kiss had happened with much less than a hug.

Before I could think of what to do, Malina made the decision for me. She leaned in and wrapped her arms around me, her head up against my chest. Naturally, I pulled her close, but the whole time I was thinking, *Don't kiss her. Don't pay attention to the way her hair smells like mangoes and she feels so good in your arms. You're sick and gross and she wouldn't want you to kiss her even if you weren't. Do. Not. Kiss. Her.*

Then she let me go, and I followed suit. Success. But wow, my bar for success had really lowered that I considered "not accidentally kissing my best friend" to be any kind of success. And that was only a partial success, because it didn't mean I didn't *want* to kiss her.

"Thank Tutu for the tea and the soup from me."

"I will. Do you think you'll be at school tomorrow?"

I shrugged. Honestly, I'd look for any excuse to get out of school, and a nose that was running like a faucet and a cough that made me sound like a pack-a-day smoker was a pretty good excuse. The only reason I'd want to be there would be to see her. But seeing her wasn't the best idea for many reasons.

"Maybe. We'll see."

"Okay. Feel better."

I put on my coat and headed out to my car. When I got there, despite the cold, I just sat in the front seat and smiled. Malina was going to the party with me. As a friend, but still. And I'd hugged her. And maybe that hug was better than the kiss because she initiated it. And I loved the way she felt in my arms.

I knew this couldn't go anywhere. I knew with my hockey and her school and what had happened between us this past week that nothing could happen with Malina. I knew all of that.

But that didn't stop me from smiling the whole way home.

Chapter Nine

MALINA

"Close," Izzy said, motioning for me to shut my eyes. "Why are you so worried about how you look for this party anyway? It's just Jackson. Unless you still aren't over that kiss?"

"I am," I said, trying not to squirm under the lie as she ran eyeliner above my right eyelashes. "It's just that it's a team party. I've never been to one of these before, so I want to make sure I look good." It had absolutely nothing to do with wanting to look good for Jackson. Nope. Not one thing.

"Whatever you say," Izzy said.

She put eyeliner on my left eye, told me to open, then leaned back a foot or two from where I was sitting on my bed to study her work. She grabbed a Q-tip and used it to fix the outside corner of my right eye, then nodded. "Perfect. You want eye shadow?"

"Whatever you think. But don't make me look like a clown."

She pulled a face at that, and dug around in her makeup

bag. Of course she'd arrived with her own tools, because the amount of makeup I owned was slim to none. The amount of makeup I wore on a regular basis was even slimmer and none-er.

"I think this color will be perfect with your complexion," she said, holding up a container of what I assumed was eye shadow. "Close."

I did, and she brushed something soft across my lids.

"So, are you nervous?" she asked.

"No. I mean, Jackson will be there the entire time. I know a lot of the guys already. Pierce is bringing his girlfriend, Lia, who I've met a few times."

"Hmm," Izzy said. "Girlfriend. Are you *sure* this isn't some kind of couples thing?"

"Positive. It's just for fun. I think Jackson knew I needed a night off as much as he does."

"If you say so. Open," she said, and immediately went after my left eye with a mascara wand.

I flinched hard. "Whoa!"

"What?"

I blinked a few times, and then opened my eye for her. "Warn a girl next time, okay? Remember, this makeup thing is still new to me."

"Sorry," Izzy said. She finished putting on the mascara, added a little blush to my cheeks, and applied some lip stain, all the while rambling about this new design for a dress she was working on. It was no surprise that she'd also begged me to let her pick my outfit for the night: a pair of leggings, a flowing shirt that was probably too thin for the Michigan weather, and my favorite pair of flats because she said they gave me more confidence than being tall yet uncomfortable in heels would.

"Okay," she said. "I think you're done." She adjusted my hair so it fell in a nice layer over my right shoulder, and then said, "You may now look in a mirror."

Even though I trusted Izzy, I still walked slowly to the bathroom down the hall, delaying the inevitable. When I got to the mirror, I did a double take. It was definitely still me, but I looked prettier. Older. More mature. More…something. The hair, the makeup, the outfit…it was all perfect.

"Well?" Izzy asked, appearing in the mirror beside me.

"You're a genius," I said, unable to hide a grin.

She brushed her shoulders off. "You know it. Okay, I should go before he gets here." She gave me a quick hug. "Text me when it's over? Or, you know, text me from there if it's lame and you need a distraction."

"Deal," I said, praying it wouldn't come to that.

"And make good choices. Don't do anything I wouldn't do."

That meant all guys were off-limits. I laughed. "Maybe. Thank you again. For all of this."

"You're welcome. Anytime."

As we walked to the door, I asked, "What are you up to tonight?"

"Well, Kylie's busy tonight, so I'm babysitting." She shrugged. "If I can't be with her, at least I can make some cash."

"That's the spirit."

"Yeah, yeah. I'll enjoy my evening with a four-year-old and six-year-old exactly as much as you'll enjoy yours, I'm sure."

I laughed. "Bye, Iz."

"Bye, Malina. Aloha, Hall family!" she called, and then headed out the front door. But she didn't get very far before she said, "Oh! Hey, Jackson."

"Hey, Izzy. Love the hair."

Though I couldn't see him yet because a wall blocked them, I could hear their conversation loud and clear.

"Thanks. Malina's inside. Have a good time tonight."

"Thanks. See ya around."

Then Jackson appeared, but stopped when he saw me.

"Hey," I said.

For a few seconds, he didn't say anything. He stood there and stared at my hair, my face, my shirt...crap. I'd told Izzy this shirt was too low cut, and now I had the proof.

"Jackson?"

"Huh?" He snapped to attention. "Oh. Sorry. Hi. You look...beautiful."

"That's all Izzy's doing," I said. "You look nice, too."

He didn't just look "nice." He looked *good*. Instead of his usual sweats or hockey attire, he was wearing tight jeans and a long-sleeve T-shirt under his USA Hockey coat. His hair, though messy as usual, looked like it might be a little more intentionally messy than normal. I forced myself to stop staring.

"Thanks," he said.

"Want to come in? I need to grab my phone." *And a sweater to cover up this shirt*, I thought.

"Sure. I'm early. We have time."

He walked inside and I closed the door behind him. "Feeling better?" I asked. He *sounded* a lot better than the last time he was over. No stuffy nose. No coughing or sneezing.

"A ton better," he said. "I swear it was Tutu's tea and soup that did the trick."

"I'm sure she'll be glad to hear that. My family's in the kitchen if you want to go say hey."

"Okay."

As soon as he walked away, I ran upstairs and dug through my dresser until I found a cardigan that somewhat matched my outfit. Izzy wouldn't approve, but what she didn't know wouldn't hurt her. I threw on the cardigan, grabbed my clutch and phone, and headed downstairs.

In the kitchen, Tutu was weaving *lauhala*, Dad was working on his laptop, and Mom was painting her nails the same deep mauve color I'd used on my nails that morning. Jackson was leaning over Tutu, asking questions about the weaving process.

My mom looked up and gasped, mid-nail-stroke. "Malina, you look so pretty!" she said. "Jackson, you should invite her to parties more often."

"Mom," I protested, hoping the powdered blush Izzy had spread on my cheeks was enough to hide my actual blush.

But Jackson smiled and said, "Gladly."

Just friends, I reminded myself as my hopes got a little too high with that comment. *He means he should invite you as a friend.*

"So what's this party you're taking my daughter to?" Dad asked.

"It's just a thing with the team and some of our friends. Very casual."

"Mmhmm," Dad said, like he didn't really believe casual parties were a thing. "Will there be drinking at this party?"

"No," he said quickly. "I mean, I don't know what some of the other guys will do. But I'll make sure Malina doesn't... that she isn't...I won't..."

"Come on, Dad. You know Jackson's a good guy," I said, saving him from having to finish the sentence he couldn't seem to find the end of.

Dad raised his eyebrows at me. "I know *he* is. It's you I'm worried about."

At that, Jackson laughed. "She does have trouble written all over her."

"Hey," I protested, nudging him with my elbow, but he just smiled at me.

"Would you like something to eat before you go?" Tutu asked.

"I don't think we have time, Tutu," I said. "Thank you, though."

"Next time," Jackson said. "And I definitely need to get the recipe for that tea you made me. Thank you again."

"*A'ole pilikia*," she said. *No problem.*

"You two have fun," Mom said.

"Be safe," Dad added.

"We will," Jackson and I said at the same time.

I grabbed my coat on the way to the car, and we headed out. It was one of the coldest nights we'd had this year, and I shivered.

"I think the pond in our yard is going to freeze to skating depths tonight," he said.

"Feels like it."

"Nothing better than lacing up an old pair of skates and hitting the ice with the snow falling down around you."

"Sounds magical," I said as we got into his car.

"You're welcome to join me anytime."

I laughed. As much as I wanted to spend time with him, Jackson knew my level of comfort with ice: I liked it in my drinks. "Oh, sure. Right before we spend a couple of hours in the emergency room with my broken femur."

"Ah, right. Let's not do that."

He put his arm on the back of my headrest so he could look behind us as he backed out of the driveway. I tried not to pay attention to how close his hand was to my neck.

"Ready for this?"

It took a second—and him putting his hand back on the steering wheel—for me to realize what "this" he was talking about. The party. Right. "Yeah," I said. "It'll be fun. There are a few new players I haven't met yet, right?"

"A few. Troy Brown is new this year. Awesome defender. Makes my job easier." He flipped on his turn signal and turned onto the main road. "And Delecky's new, but you met him after a game earlier this season, right?"

"Number fifty? Looks like he should be on a surfboard instead of hockey skates?"

"Yeah. That's him. I think you know everyone else from last year. I'm sure some of the girls will be new, though."

"Is Matthews still dating Lauren? I haven't seen her in his Snapchats lately."

"Nah, they broke up. She couldn't deal with his travel schedule or something."

Dealing with travel schedules *was* hard. I had to keep reminding myself of that and the fact that I got so much more work done when he was traveling. Tonight would be fun, but then it was back to reality. "Too bad. I really liked her. Is he okay?"

He shrugged. "Seems to be. I roomed with him during our last trip, and he wasn't crying into his pillow or anything."

I laughed. "Well, in that case, I'm sure he's completely fine."

"Come on, you know we don't talk about stuff like that like you girls do."

"Yeah, yeah. I know." I paused for a second and toyed with a loose thread on the sleeve of my coat. "Hey, Jackson?"

"Yeah?"

"Thanks for inviting me to this. I need a night off."

In the dim light of the streetlights, I saw him smile one more time. "I know you do. You're welcome." Then he kept driving.

Chapter Ten

Jackson

The party was already in full swing when we arrived. It was dark inside, the only light coming from a few low lamps in corners. Music was playing loudly, but not too loud for me to miss the cheers of, "Jackson!" as I nudged the door shut behind us. I gave a few waves and fist bumps. Malina hung close by, but gave hugs to the guys she knew and was friendly while meeting the ones she didn't.

"Want to go get a drink?" I asked, leaning close so she could hear me over the music. Damn, she smelled good. That, combined with how she looked—the outfit and makeup Izzy had put her in, no doubt—were probably going to be the death of me that night.

She nodded, and I led her toward the kitchen, stopping to toss our coats on a pile on the stairs on the way. It was quieter in the kitchen, and brighter with a light on over the table. A few of the guys were sitting around the table with a deck of cards dealt between them.

"Jackson!" Pierce called the second I walked into the room.

He was standing up against the counter, which was completely covered in beverages. He was holding hands with Lia, which I'd give him crap about if the girl didn't make him so damn happy. Since she was a figure skater, I was used to seeing her hair in a bun at the ice arena, but she looked pretty with it loose around her shoulders. *Not as pretty as Malina, though*, I found myself thinking. Pierce let go of her hand long enough to give me and Malina quick hugs, and Lia did the same a second later.

"Long time no see," Pierce said to Malina.

"Right? It's been a while. Heard you've had a few good games lately."

Pierce grinned. "Yeah. It's been fun. Hard work has paid off."

I nodded toward the beverages. "What are we drinking tonight?"

"Pro tip," Lia said. "Don't pick the red stuff. It tastes like cough syrup."

"I'll learn from your mistakes," Malina said. "I'll have pop."

I grabbed two cups and poured one for each of us. Then I motioned Malina toward the kitchen table. "You guys remember my friend Malina?" I asked.

That was answered with rounds of greetings from the guys who already knew her. Troy Brown, one of the new additions to the team, set his cards facedown and stood to shake Malina's hand.

"Hey, I'm Troy."

"Malina. Nice to meet you."

"Malina?" he asked. "That's a beautiful name."

Maybe it was the way he said the word "beautiful." Maybe it was the way he clearly checked her out before returning to his seat. Maybe it was his smile, which was bigger than when we won a game in overtime at the buzzer. Whatever it was, it made the hair on the back of my neck stand on end.

Malina smiled back, apparently oblivious to my concerns. "Thank you."

"You guys want to play?" Matthews asked, motioning to two empty folding chairs that had been pulled up to the table.

"What are you playing?" I asked.

"Fooligan," Matthews said.

"Not sure I know how to play that one," Malina said.

Before I could say anything, she took one of the empty seats. The one right next to Troy. Definitely not wanting to leave her alone with him, I took the seat next to her.

"Oh, it's easy," Troy said. He handed her a few cards from the top of the deck without counting them, and then did the same for me. "You'll catch on. It's Matthews' turn."

All eyes were on Matthews. He studied his hand for a long time, then put down two cards: a two and a seven. One red, the other black.

Troy scratched his chin.

Though I hadn't been playing hockey with him longer than a few months, I could read him and Matthews well enough to know that this Fooligan game was complete bullshit.

"Ah ha," Troy said before laying down a card. The ten of clubs.

"Nice play," Delecky said. "Nice play." Then he studied his own hand. He scratched the top of his head. After a deep breath, he laid down his entire hand, seven cards, faceup and said, "Fooligan."

"Aw, man," Matthews said. "Tough luck, Troy. Gotta drink." He handed Troy a cup of what appeared to be the red stuff Lia had warned us against.

Troy took it like a champ and then turned to Malina. "Your turn."

This was one of the things I loved about Malina. She was smart. She'd been studying the cards, trying to figure out what kind of complicated logic they were using to play this ridiculous game. But she was also smart enough to pick up on their bullshit and go with it. That was one of the things that made her so different from the girls I'd dated. She glanced over at me before clutching her cards close to her chest.

"Are you looking at my hand, Jackson?"

I smiled and held up my non-card-holding hand in a gesture of innocence. "I would never!"

She smiled back before proudly laying two cards faceup on the table: the three of diamonds and the queen of spades.

"Wow," Matthews said.

"Beginner's luck," Delecky said, gathering all of the faceup cards on the table and passing them to Malina, as if she'd actually done something good.

Malina beamed at me. My stomach gave a little flip. She was so pretty when she beamed.

"You're up, Jackson," Matthews said.

I looked at my hand and picked a card at random: the jack of diamonds. I placed it on the table, and was immediately greeted by a chorus of booing.

"That was a terrible play," Troy said.

"It's like you don't even know Fooligan," Delecky added.

"I think he should have to drink for that nonsense," Matthews said.

Thankfully, at that moment, Pierce walked over and clapped me hard on both shoulders. I think sometimes the guy forgot I wasn't wearing my goalie pads.

"Hey, man. Be my partner for beer pong?" he asked.

I pulled my keys out of my pocket and waved them in the air. "Can't. I'm driving."

Pierce shrugged. "We don't lose, you don't drink. We were undefeated last time. Gotta keep up our record."

I considered. On the one hand, I was deeply competitive, and couldn't resist the lure of maintaining an undefeated record, especially when the alternative was the distinctly non-competitive Fooligan. But on the other hand, I really didn't want to leave Malina. I glanced over at her, but she was laughing with Troy over something I'd missed. Whoa. Jealousy struck hard and fast, right at the center of my chest.

"I'll take your place," Lia said, leaning over to take the cards out of my hand before I could stop her. "And I'll keep Malina company while you two play."

Pierce kissed the top of Lia's head. "See? Perfect."

"What's perfect?" Malina asked.

"I'm taking Jackson's place so he can go play beer pong with Pierce," Lia explained, nudging me out of my seat. "Apparently I'm not the partner he's looking for."

Pierce laughed. "Lia, I love you, but last time we played, you didn't even hit the table, let alone one of the cups. Stick to figure skating."

I turned to Malina. "You good here?" *Please say no, please say no, please say no.*

"Yes. I, unlike you, am extremely good at Fooligan. Go play. Have fun."

I'd look like a jerk if I didn't go after that. After one last second of hesitation, I turned and followed Pierce.

"So, how's it going?" Pierce asked once we were out of earshot from the girls. "Everything back to status quo with you two?"

"Yeah," I said, but didn't meet Pierce's eyes when I said it.

"She looks hot tonight." Then he quickly held up his hands in innocence. "I mean that in the most 'I already have a girlfriend' kind of way."

I waved off his concern. "It's fine. She does look hot."

"Just friends, huh?"

When I looked at him, he was studying me beneath that stupid all-knowing raised eyebrow of his.

"Just friends," I said, even though it was a total lie.

Yep. Completely screwed.

Chapter Eleven

MALINA

"So, are you a figure skater too, or is that only Lia?" Troy asked.

I laughed. "I'm definitely not a figure skater. I'm lucky if I can walk in a straight line without falling down."

Troy grinned at me. Across the table, Matthews shuffled the cards, ready for another round of Fooligan.

"Nice. So you're not a figure skater. What are you into?"

"Not a lot," I said.

"Don't let her fool you. She's a genius," Lia said as she picked up the cards that were dealt to her. "She's a science and technology wizard."

"Really?" Troy asked. "STEM stuff? Did you go to regionals last year?"

"I went to watch, but I didn't compete. My project wasn't ready. Why, did you?" As soon as the words were out of my mouth, I wanted to take them back. Of course a hockey player talented enough to be on NTDP wouldn't be into STEM.

Hockey players thought that kind of stuff was nerdy. Well, not Jackson, but only because I'd brainwashed him before hockey completely took over his life. But then Troy surprised me.

"Yeah. Did you see the power-assisted dog wheelchair?"

Of *course* I'd seen it. I was pretty sure everyone there had seen it, in addition to the world's most adorable three-legged dog, who used it to get around without a problem. Was I really talking to the inventor? "No way. That was *you*?"

Troy grinned. "Lucy is the greatest dog ever, despite only having 75 percent of her limbs."

"She's adorable," I said. "And that wheelchair was amazing. How did you come up with that?"

He shrugged and toyed with the card in his hand. Across the table, someone either made a really good or a really terrible Fooligan move, so he looked up at them for a second before turning back to me. "A lot of prototypes. The very first one wasn't electronic at all, and was mostly made out of old rollerblade parts. It was okay, but she still struggled to get around sometimes. I knew I could make it better, so I did."

My heart warmed. That was what I loved about STEM. Improving someone else's life, even a dog's life. Seeing the opportunity to make something, and then making it. Going from idea to actuality. Meeting someone else who understood that was the best.

Troy, Lia, and I all took our Fooligan turns, Troy suffering through a swig of the terrible red stuff that made him shiver this time.

"Are you submitting anything for competition this year?" I asked.

He shrugged one shoulder. "Probably not. I tinkered with a few things, but with hockey being so busy…"

I nodded. I couldn't imagine Jackson ever having the time to do a STEM project, and knew Troy had to be in the same position.

"What about you?" Lia asked. "Did you finish your project? Are you submitting it?"

Guilt washed over me as I thought about my project. "It's not finished yet. I'm not sure I'll be able to get it to work. If I do, I'll definitely compete, though. There's so much scholarship money on the line this year. Even more than last year."

Troy waved this comment off. "There's so much pressure for the scholarship money. Too much. Enter because you want to enter. Because you're proud of what you've done. What are you working on?"

My cheeks flushed, and I hoped the lights in there were dim enough to hide it. "It's this model of the solar system."

"Malina's going to be an astrophysicist," Lia said.

Clearly the girl had been brainwashed by Pierce, who had been brainwashed by Jackson.

"That's awesome. Tell me more about this model solar system," Troy said.

"Well, it's completely to scale," I said, and immediately wanted to suck the words right back where they came from. Of course a model in a STEM competition would be to scale. I couldn't believe I was saying that to the guy who'd won one of the categories last year. "And each of the planets has a bulb to show the amount of light it reflects from the sun. And then I made an app where you can rotate it to show different times throughout the year."

"Troy, your turn," Matthews said, tossing a few cards in his direction.

Troy waved him off and kept his attention on me. "Wow. That's really cool."

He sounded genuinely impressed, but I was not that impressive. "Maybe, but it doesn't work right. I can't get the rotation and the lighting to work at the same time."

"Isn't that the fun of it?" he asked. "The challenge?"

The spark in his eye when he said the words reminded me

that it *was* a challenge. He was right. I worried so much about scholarships and getting into college that I forgot the project was a challenge itself. Making it happen was supposed to be fun.

Before I could say anything in response, Matthews tossed another card and hit Troy right in the forehead. "Dude. It's your turn. You're holding up Fooligan. As punishment, I think you have to refill all of our drinks," Matthews said, holding up his own empty red cup.

Troy rolled his eyes at me before getting up and snatching the cup out of Matthews's hand. "Fine, but only because I'm thirsty, too. Can I get you two anything?" he asked Lia and me.

We both told him we were okay.

"Be right back," he said. "Don't let them skip my turn."

Once he was out of earshot, Lia leaned closer to me. "Oh my gosh, you two would be *perfect* together."

I glanced back at Troy, but tried to hide it in case he was looking. I realized that, for the first time since the kiss, I wasn't thinking about Jackson. That had to say something about Troy, right? "You think?"

"Yes! You're both into the same things and he seems really nice, and…" She surreptitiously glanced over her shoulder, too. "He's cute, don't you think?"

To be honest, I hadn't really noticed or thought about it. He looked…well, he looked like most of the guys on the NTDP team. Which meant he looked like Jackson—pale, tall, muscular from endless hockey drills. But he did have that grin with those perfect teeth. And it was adorable the way he lit up when he was talking about STEM stuff…

"Yeah," I finally said. "He is."

Lia smiled. "I thought so. Okay. Go with me on this. I'm going to make sure you guys get some time alone to talk, okay? Or…whatever else you want to do alone."

"Stop," I said, swatting at her with my cards, but she just laughed.

At that moment, Troy returned, several cups in his hands. He passed them around the table and returned to his seat. "What did I miss?" he asked.

"Nothing," Lia said quickly. Too quickly.

Then she winked so only I could see it.

Alone with Troy. Was that something I wanted? I guessed I was about to find out.

It turned out Lia's plan was easier in theory than in practice, and the reason was my best friend. Once Jackson finished his game with Pierce, he returned and became weirdly clingy. Like as much as Lia wanted Troy and me to be alone, that was exactly how much Jackson didn't want to let me out of his sight. That was how we ended up spending a lot of the time at the party as a group of five—me, Jackson, Troy, Lia, and Pierce—with occasional other teammates and friends coming in and out as the night went on.

It was fun. I hadn't relaxed or laughed this much in a long time. Jackson was right. A night off was exactly what I needed. It was clear all of the guys needed a night off, too. The bonding they'd done on the ice carried over to the party, and they laughed and shared inside jokes and let loose, with Pierce at the center of attention, and Jackson a pretty close second by association.

"Hey, Pierce, Jackson," Lia said over the music. "Some of the guys need help moving the furniture in the bonus room. Can you two help?"

It was so obvious the way she said it—you *two*. Not including Troy. Giving him the opportunity to stay behind with me. Thankfully, she'd played right into both Pierce's and

Jackson's hands. "Which wimps can't move the furniture by themselves?" Jackson asked.

"Ones who need us to bring in the big guns," Pierce said, standing and motioning for Jackson to follow him.

Jackson stood, but then looked back at me. "I'll be right back, okay?"

"Fine," I said, probably too quickly. "I'll be right here."

Jackson gave one last look at Troy before walking away.

"Don't hurt yourself," I called. They would never hear the end of it from their coach if one of them broke their foot by dropping a couch on it or something.

Troy took this opportunity to sit next to me on the couch in the place Jackson had vacated. He smelled good, like some kind of body spray that I could really get used to.

"I'm glad they're doing that," he said. "Practices lately have been brutal. I'm sore. I don't know how they aren't."

"They've had one more year than you to get used to being on the team and the practices that go with it."

"True."

"Did you not try for the team last year?" I asked.

He shook his head. "I thought I was going to be happy playing for my high school, playing for a college, but then I watched their undefeated season last year and saw all of the interest they were getting from the scouts—especially Pierce—and I felt like I was missing out on something. Like I should try it, too. So I did, and I made it. I don't get to play nearly as much as I did on my high school team, but it's worth it. I love this team."

"Except for the soreness from practices," I said.

He laughed and rolled his shoulders. "Except that."

"But you don't have any time to do STEM stuff? Your invention was pretty great." Did I sound too overenthusiastic and fangirl-ish? I was so bad at this kind of thing.

He shrugged. "I dabble in stuff when we're not on the

road. When I have time. But I also know this is my season to play hockey. I won't be able to play forever. Maybe no NHL teams or colleges will want me. Maybe I'll get hurt and won't be able to play anymore. Then I'll have all the time in the world to invent stuff. I have to go with this while I can."

"You're smart," I said.

"Yeah, well you're smart and pretty," he said back.

I fought back a cringe, torn between being flattered and appalled by his poor flirting skills. That's what he was doing, or what he thought he was doing, right? Flirting? "Thanks," I said, and picked at a loose thread on the arm of the couch.

"Hey, do you want to go out with me sometime?"

The thread slipped between my fingers. Terrible flirting? Okay. Getting to know each other there? Okay. But a date? "I…" I automatically reached for an excuse. I didn't date much. After watching Jackson go through what he went through, the last thing I wanted was to be one of those girls. He dated enough for both of us. Plus about seven more people.

But then there was Jackson. Maybe the best way to get my mind off him and the kiss was to go out with someone else. Troy and I would have plenty to talk about. He seemed nice. One date couldn't hurt anything, could it? I took a deep breath. "Okay," I said. "That sounds good."

He grinned. "Perfect. Dinner?"

"It's a date."

Chapter Twelve

JACKSON

"What are they doing?" I asked, peering around the corner to try to see Troy and Malina.

"Ouch," Pierce said when my distraction caused the couch we were carrying to bang against his leg. "Pay attention!"

"Sorry," I said, hoisting the couch up higher again. We were moving it to the hall so the room it had been in could be used for some kind of human Hungry Hungry Hippos game. When it came to my teammates, there were just some things I didn't ask about. But Troy was not one of those things. Not when Malina was involved. "But really. What's Troy doing with Malina?"

"Why do you care?" Lia asked. "Troy's a good guy, and it's not like you're trying to date her."

I tried not to scowl as we squeezed through the doorframe. She was right. At least I thought so. Was she right? "So this furniture-moving adventure was your plan to get the two of them alone?"

"Nope," Lia said innocently. "I didn't have anything to do with Hungry Hungry Hippos."

"Let's set it down," Pierce said. "And also, Lia is a terrible liar."

"Hey," she said, slipping herself under his now-free arm. "Need I remind you that I hid my true identity from you for weeks when we first met?"

Using their distraction to my advantage, I slipped away, more than ready to head back to Malina.

"Jackson," Lia said before I could get very far.

Reluctantly, I turned back to her. "Yeah?"

"He's a nice guy. She's a nice girl. They have a lot in common. I don't know why you seem not cool with this, but be cool, okay?"

"Cool," I echoed. "Yeah. Okay." I could do that. Maybe.

When I got back to Malina and Troy, she was laughing over something he'd said. People saw red when they got angry. Did they see green when they got jealous? If so, things were starting to look a little lime-like. There was a tiny bit of space between them, but not enough for me to slip into and sit without looking like a complete douche. I settled for sitting on the edge of the couch, to Malina's left. We'd been there a while, but I could still smell the mango scent of her hair.

"What's so funny?" I asked.

"Troy," Malina said. "You didn't tell me he was funny."

"Hey," I said, wanting to send the conversation in a different direction, wanting to move Malina away from this couch to a place where the space between her and Troy was bigger. "Want to go watch human Hungry Hungry Hippos? It sounds ridiculous."

"Watch?" Troy said, jumping to his feet. "I want to play! Come on, Malina. Cheer me on?"

Clearly I should have been more specific about *only* inviting Malina.

"Sure," she said, getting to her feet and following Troy before I could stop her. I sighed and followed, feeling not only like a loser, but also a jerk.

Human Hungry Hungry Hippos, it turned out, involved those four-wheeled seated scooters from elementary school and most of the balls from the ball pit in Matthews's little sister's princess castle. It was actually funny to watch, but instead of playing, I chose to stay behind with Malina, who seemed to only have eyes for Troy.

Once the games were over and the couch had been returned to its rightful place, I glanced at the clock on my phone. I needed to get Malina home soon if I wanted to stay in her parents' good graces. Which I did.

"Ready to get going?" I asked, leaning close both so that Malina could hear me over the music and so Troy *couldn't* hear me over the music.

Malina pressed the home button on her phone and nodded when she saw the time. She leaned over to Troy and motioned toward me with one hand. "I gotta go. Curfew."

Troy frowned, but nodded. When he stood, it was his turn to say something to Malina that I couldn't hear. I wasn't a fan of when the tables were turned. But then he turned to me.

"Jackson, good to see you. Thanks for introducing me to Malina."

He reached out for a first bump, but it wasn't really his knuckles I wanted to punch.

Malina gave him a little wave, and then we grabbed our coats and headed out of the party into the cold, quiet night air.

"That was nice," Malina said as she wrapped her thick winter coat tighter around her against the wind. "Thanks for inviting me."

I knew I should have said, "You're welcome," but my brain wasn't into "should"s at that moment. "What's up with you and Troy?" I asked before we even reached the car.

Malina glanced over at me, eyebrows raised.

Okay, maybe my tone was a little more…intense than it needed to be for that question.

We got in the car. She buckled her seat belt before saying anything.

"He's nice," she said. "We have a lot in common."

I pulled away from the curb and headed down the street. "And?"

"And?" she asked. "And what?"

"And is something going to happen between you two?"

It took a long time before she said anything. Too long. Each second and each streetlight that ticked by was too much.

Finally, she turned in her seat toward me. She ran a hand through her long, dark hair. "Have I ever once given you crap about any of the girls you've hung out with?"

This tone wasn't one I heard from her often. Malina was usually so calm, so even-tempered. This wasn't usually. The fact that she was both angry and correct made me cringe. There had been a lot of girls. And she hadn't given me crap about any of them. "No," I said, glancing over her shoulder toward my blind spot as I switched lanes.

"Exactly. But you're giving me crap about the *one* guy I want to go out with, who happens to be your friend?"

"Well, yeah, but—"

"Is he a murderer? Is he going to drug me and date rape me? Does he have some kind of weird fetish I should know about?"

As much as I wanted to say "yes" to all three of those, I couldn't. Troy was a good guy. Not good for *her*, but still. "No. He's fine."

"Then I don't see what the problem is. The only other reason I can think that you wouldn't want me to go out with him would be if you wanted to go out with me instead. But that's not right. You don't want to go out with me."

I tightened my grip on the steering wheel. It was a statement, but I wanted it to be a question. I wanted to disagree. I wanted to lean over and kiss her again and make her forget all about Troy. But I couldn't.

Instead, I blurted out, "He snores. A lot. And he gets toothpaste all over the sink and he wears socks to bed and consistently sleeps through his alarm."

Even though I was looking out the windshield, not at Malina, I could feel her staring, eyes burning holes right through me. It was too late to take the words back, but that didn't mean I didn't want to. I was such an idiot.

"Okay," she said, slowly. "I don't think any of those things are going to be a problem on the first date, but I will take them under advisement."

"Good."

"And maybe you shouldn't room with him while traveling anymore."

That list wasn't even that bad. All of us on the team had quirks and habits that could drive everyone else crazy. That was why we switched up roommates all the time. Yeah, it was so we'd get to know one another, but it was also so we didn't kill one another over who kept the hotel room too hot or too cold, sang terribly in the shower, or left smelly hockey socks all over the floor.

"Maybe," I said.

I turned onto her street, and we fell into silence for a little while.

"Tonight was fun," she finally said after a sigh. "Human Hungry Hungry Hippos was kind of brilliant. I needed a night to laugh like that."

Crap. This really was my fault. Not only did the party introduce her to Troy, but it probably also made her realize how much she needed another night out, like a date with him. "Glad you had a good time," I said, wondering if my tone gave away how I really felt. I pulled into her driveway. A couple of lights were still on in the house. "Are your parents waiting up for you?"

Malina studied the house. "It's probably Tutu. She's a night owl."

"Tell her I said good night."

"I will. Thanks again for the ride and the invite."

Get out of the car. Walk her to the door. Kiss her like you want to. "You're welcome. Good night." *Or just sit here like a complete and utter failure.*

Malina quietly closed the car door and walked toward the porch. I leaned my head on the steering wheel and wondered how tonight had gone quite so terribly.

Then I got an idea. I pulled my phone out of my pocket and opened a new text message to Troy.

Me: *Are you going out with Malina?*

The ellipses that showed he was typing appeared almost immediately.

Troy: *Yeah. Dinner sometime while we're in town. That cool?*

"Cool" wasn't the word I'd use. The thought of him picking her up, taking her to a restaurant, telling her all about his stupid STEM invention that I knew absolutely nothing about, then dropping her off and kissing her, putting his hands all over her…

Nope.

No way.

He wanted to go out with her?

Fine.

But I was going, too.

Me: *Let's double date.*

Not a question. No opportunity for him to say no.

Troy: *Sounds good.*

Troy: *Who are you going to bring?*

Me: *Someone from school. Krista.*

Had I asked Krista out yet? No. But would she say yes? Probably. The only reason I hadn't gone out with her before was because I'd dated her best friend, and it hadn't ended well—I'd gotten over her a little quicker than she'd gotten over me. All of my attempts to casually flirt with Krista since then had been shot down. But that was sophomore year. Her friend was dating someone else, and they looked to be one of those "start dating in high school and eventually get married" kind of couples. We'd all changed since sophomore year. Krista would probably be willing to go out with me now. I'd make it clear I only wanted something casual. Just a fun night out. I'd treat her well. Buy her dinner. And I'd get to keep an eye on Malina and Troy the whole time.

Troy: *Cool. I'll let you know the plan.*

Me: *Thanks.*

Then I switched out of my text messages and into a social media app where I knew I followed Krista. I opened a new message in the app.

Me: *Hey. Looking for someone to go on a double date*

with me. Interested?

Even though she wasn't the person I really *wanted* to be asking out, I still held my breath while waiting for her response. After all, getting shot down was getting shot down, no matter the reason for asking someone out. Thankfully, I didn't have to wait long.

Krista: *Random…but sure. Fill me in at school Monday?*

I said I would and threw my phone on the passenger seat before backing out of Malina's driveway.

Was I being a jerk? Probably. Selfish? Absolutely.

But right at that moment, I cared about Malina more than any of that.

Chapter Thirteen

"So, how far are you going to go tonight?" Izzy asked. "First base? Second? Fifth?"

I was sitting on the couch next to Izzy, scrolling through Instagram so I'd have something to do with my hands. "Pretty sure there are only four bases. Or three, plus home."

"Oh, right. Of course guys would choose an analogy with only three steps before sex. Girls have at least five." She looked up at the ceiling and counted off on her fingers, doing some kind of math. "No, six. And we *especially* enjoy number three."

I refrained from asking for clarification. "Whatever you say. Does that mean things are going well with Kylie?"

"Yeah. It's hard because she isn't out to her family or most of her friends yet, but we can work with that. She's the kind of beautiful that doesn't need makeup, and she's so sweet—did I tell you that she volunteers every week at the Ronald McDonald House?—and she's funny without trying, and did

I mention she's absolutely gorgeous? Lina…"

Uh oh. I knew what was coming. Yes, Izzy and Kylie had only gone out a couple of times, but there was no other way Izzy knew how to finish that sentence.

"…I think I'm falling in love with her."

Yep. That was my Izzy. The girl fell hard and fast. I only hoped Kylie didn't get freaked out or take advantage of it or any of the many other things Izzy's exes had done. It was a true testament to Izzy's character that she was still hopeful and optimistic enough to fall so freely after all she'd been through. Yes, she took breakups hard, but then she bounced back.

"Have you told her that?" I asked, switching over to Snapchat.

"Not yet. Maybe this weekend. I'm sure we'll do something romantic. She told me about this little art museum in her town that she wants to show me around. And she knows one of the artists, because of course she does." Izzy sighed. "Perfect girl is perfect."

I looked over at her and smiled. Every time she went through a breakup, I wondered if she'd get back to this place again. If she'd make it through the tears back to this smile. "You're happy."

"I am. And you? Tell me about this Troy character. Is he gorgeous? Do you like his…Adam's apple? His narrow hips and big calves?"

I laughed. "You really have zero clue what it's like to be straight, don't you?"

"Possibly even less than zero."

Thoughts of Troy didn't fill me with the same tingles as thoughts of Jackson had lately, but that didn't mean anything. Tingles took time. "I only met him once, but he was nice. And cute."

"Cute? Not gorgeous?"

I looked up from my phone and tried to picture Troy in my mind. "I don't know. He looks like a hockey player, I guess."

"Like Jackson?"

Jackson, on the other hand, was easy to picture. Too easy. "No, a little different from Jackson. I don't know. His picture's on the NTDP website if you really want to see him."

"Fine. So what did you like about him when you met him? What made you willing to go out with him?"

"Well, he was really nice, and he used to be into STEM before he got into hockey, so we have a lot in common. And he was funny. And…" If I were being honest, the real reason I agreed to go out with him was because of how interested he seemed in me, and how I thought doing so might help me get my mind off Jackson. But saying any of that out loud, even to Izzy, felt wrong, so I kept my mouth shut.

"And you're hoping to get to know him more tonight so you can decide if you're really into him or if agreeing to go out with him was a terrible, drunk decision?"

"I wasn't drunk," I said.

"But I'm right about the rest," Izzy said.

I didn't disagree.

The doorbell rang. I froze and pressed the home button to see the time on my phone. "That's him." Suddenly, I hated the crewneck shirt I was wearing, desperately needed more lip stain, and wanted to rewash, dry, and straighten my hair just so I could delay this and make sure I was perfect before seeing him. Why did people think this dating thing was fun? "I'm not ready," I said. "I need to fix my hair."

Izzy stopped my hand midair on its way to my scalp. "No you don't. You're perfect, and even if you weren't, he'd only be worth it if he thought you were anyway."

"But I have that paper due, and I already took one night off to go to the party, and now I'm taking tonight off? I'm going to fail my classes and—"

"Malina." Izzy put both hands on my shoulders. "You're far from failing any of your classes. It's one night. This is why I'm here, remember? To prevent this last-minute freak-out we both knew you were going to have. Come on."

She stood, took my hand, and pulled hard enough that I wasn't positive my arm was going to stay in its socket. My parents had taken Tutu to a doctor appointment in Ann Arbor and weren't back yet, so Izzy had volunteered to be the approval/send-off committee. She motioned for me to open the door, which I did. But then I froze. It wasn't Troy standing on my front porch. It was Jackson.

For a second, my brain struggled with this. It had been Troy who asked me out, not Jackson, right? The whole point of this thing, or most of the point of this thing, was to get my mind *off* Jackson. But seeing him standing on my front porch, dressed in his nicest pair of jeans and a button-up shirt with the sleeves rolled up to the elbows despite the cold, my mind wasn't off him. Not even a little bit.

"Jackson," Izzy said. "What are you doing here?"

Apparently her lips weren't frozen shut from shock like mine were.

But Jackson wasn't looking at Izzy. He was looking at me. "You look beautiful," he said.

"Duh," Izzy said. "Of course she does. But that doesn't explain what you're doing here. Where's this punk Troy?"

"Right here," Troy said, jogging up.

I forced my attention to him. He was wearing dark jeans and a gray polo shirt. He was also carrying a rose, which he held out to me.

"Sorry," he said. "I forgot this in the car."

The feel of one of the thorns against my thumb snapped me back to reality. Troy. I was going out with Troy. He brought me a rose. I held it up to my nose and smelled the petals.

"It's beautiful. Thank you," I said.

"You're welcome."

Izzy held out a hand to Troy. "I'm Malina's friend Izzy."

"Nice to meet you."

"You too. And the rose is sweet and all, but I still don't understand why there's two of you and only one Malina. Is this some kind of polyamorous thing? Because you know I'll be the last person to judge anyone's preferences, but it seems like—"

"You didn't tell her," Jackson said, turning to Troy. "I thought you were going to tell her."

Troy held up his hands in innocence. "I thought *you* were going to tell her. This was your idea, so it was your job."

"Tell me what?" I asked, looking back and forth between the two.

"That this is a double date," Troy said.

Oh. I'd been on a couple of double dates and group dates before, and they were actually fun. But wait. A knot started to form in the pit of my stomach. If this was a double date and Jackson was the other guy, that meant there was going to be another girl. That meant I was going to have to sit and watch him smile at and flirt with some other girl. Could I really do that?

"Where's your girl?" Izzy asked. "Or guy," she added quickly. "Again, don't want to make any assumptions."

"Oh, trust me," Jackson said. "You and I are still working with the same half of the population. We're picking Krista up on the way to the restaurant."

"Didn't you already date Krista?" Izzy asked.

Jackson shook his head. "Nope. Kristy with both a -y and an -ie, but never Krista."

Izzy rolled her eyes. "Oh, right. My mistake."

"Krista Crawford?" I asked. I didn't mean for my voice to sound incredulous, but it did. He liked *her*? The girl's personality was as exciting as a piece of Wonder bread. She was pretty, though. Prettier than me. Was that why he liked her?

"Yeah. Is that okay?" he asked me.

No. No, no, no. It wasn't okay. Not at all. But I forced a smile and, as casually as I could muster, said, "Sure." Then I handed the rose to Izzy to take care of for me and turned to Troy. My date for the evening. The guy I was going to have to stay focused on all night. "Ready to go?"

He grinned. "Ready. Nice to meet you, Izzy."

"Have her home by 6:30," Izzy said.

"It's already 6:02, and this isn't your home," I said.

"Oh, right. Then I guess have fun."

"Thanks," I said and gave her a quick hug.

"Later, Izzy," Jackson said. "Next time we'll have to do a triple date."

Izzy wrinkled her nose. "A threesome with you? No thank you."

Then before Jackson could respond, she nudged me out the door and closed it behind us, no doubt going to eat some of the *malsadas* Tutu left on the counter with her name on them.

"You look beautiful," Troy said as we walked down the sidewalk to Jackson's car.

His arm brushed against mine, and I hoped to feel that jolt, that first date jittery excitement, but I didn't feel a thing. Maybe the surprise of seeing Jackson was still too much for me.

"Thanks. You look nice, too."

"What about me?" Jackson asked. "Don't I look nice?"

Thankfully, Troy stepped in before I had to respond. "Dude, she's *my* date. Quit that."

I let them argue while I climbed into the backseat of the car. The familiar smell of Jackson's cologne washed over me, and I kind of hated myself for how much I liked it.

"How was practice today?" I asked, hoping to get us all back on neutral ground.

Troy groaned. "Coach wasn't there, so he had Pierce run practice."

I grinned. That couldn't have been good. "How are his practice-leading skills?"

"Intense. He made us do this drill called the iron cross. I'm pretty sure it got that name because you spend the entire time praying for it to be over."

"Seriously," Jackson said. "I'm not sure if I'm going to be able to walk tomorrow."

"Oh, are you out of shape? Maybe your backup goalie will have to start the next game," I teased.

I expected Jackson to joke back. To say something about how the other goalie would start a game when hell froze over, but he didn't.

Instead, he said, "Nice, Malina. Real nice."

My stomach clenched. "I was kidding."

"He's just jealous that I'm currently the only one in the car with a date," Troy said, reaching forward to lightly punch Jackson's arm. "He'll be better once we pick up Krista. Right, man?"

"Right," Jackson muttered, but it didn't sound very convincing at all.

Chapter Fourteen

JACKSON

The table was part of the problem. The waitress couldn't have seated us at a rectangular table, where I could sit across from Krista and next to Troy, leaving Malina safely in the corner of my vision. No, she seated us at a tiny square table. Krista had taken the seat to my left, and Malina had taken the seat to my right, which was close enough that I could smell the warm vanilla sugar on her skin and she could brush up against my arm when she reached for her water glass. If I were on a date with her, this wouldn't be a problem. It would be perfect. I wanted it to be perfect. But it wasn't perfect because I was sitting across the table from Troy, which meant I had to look at him all night.

"How's your salad?" I asked Krista.

Because yeah. Maybe a gigantic chunk of my attention was on Malina and Troy, but I'd asked Krista out. I was going to treat her well.

She gave me a funny look, fork poised over her salad

plate. "You asked me that same question two minutes ago."

Crap. I did? I didn't remember asking her, and I definitely didn't remember her answer. "Sorry," I said. "Still good?"

She smiled. She was pretty, the light over our table making her dark brown hair shine. She wasn't Malina-pretty or anything, but still.

"The salad's good. Everything's good." She gave my arm a light squeeze. "Relax, okay?"

Perfect. She thought I was nervous. I could work with that. I smiled at her once more before picking up my fork and diving back into my salad. I really was starving after today's practice.

"So, Malina," Troy said. "Your grandma's from Hawaii?"

"Tutu," I said, my mouth still full of salad.

Troy gave me a strange look.

I swallowed and said, "That's the Hawaiian word for 'grandma.' Tutu."

He gave me a less-than-pleased look before turning back to Malina. "So, Tutu's from Hawaii?"

Malina dabbed at the corners of her mouth with her napkin. "Yes. My mom, too. My dad's from Michigan, but he went to the University of Hawaii, which is where my parents met."

"Is your name Hawaiian?" Krista asked. "It's so pretty."

Malina nodded. "It means calming or soothing. And thanks."

"Your name isn't the only thing that's pretty," Troy said, as one hand disappeared beneath the table.

I swallowed wrong and was pretty sure a piece of lettuce got lodged in my left lung. Who did Troy think he was, saying shit like that? And what was he doing with his hand? As I coughed, Krista put a hand on my back and gave me my glass of water.

"You okay?" she asked.

I took a drink, coughed again, and nodded. "Fine," I said, then cleared my throat when the word came out wrong. "I'm fine. Sorry."

"Have you been to Hawaii?" Troy asked, ignoring my distress.

"A few times, yeah. It's really beautiful."

"But you've never been to Canada," I said. "We've been to Canada, and it's beautiful, too. Probably more beautiful than Hawaii."

Troy gave me a pretty clear "what the hell are you talking about?" look. "Well, I've never been to Hawaii, but I'm pretty sure that's a false statement. Canada's cold and gray most of the year. And the only things we've really seen are the insides of ice arenas and hotels. You can't possibly tell me you think that's better than Hawaii."

I shrugged. "Maybe it is." Even as the words came out of my mouth, I knew I was being ridiculous, but I couldn't help it. I didn't want Troy thinking Malina was some kind of exotic beauty from some incredible place. Even though she was.

Malina practically burned holes in my skin with her WTF look. Then she cleared her throat and turned to my left. "So, Krista. You have PE with Coach Green after me, right? Third period?"

Krista groaned and put her head dramatically in her hands. "Rhythmic. Gymnastics. I can't believe she's making us do rhythmic gymnastics."

Troy laughed. "Seriously? That's something I'd like to see."

Unlike Troy, who didn't go to our school, that was something I *could* see. "Second and third period?" I asked. "I'll stop by tomorrow. I'll find some reason I need to be in the gym." Then I turned to Krista. "As much as you hate it, I'm sure you're a fantastic rhythmic gymnast."

Krista laughed. "Thanks, but I'm no athlete like you. It

really is laughable."

"Do you know who's amazing at gymnastics?" Malina asked.

My stomach churned. No. She wouldn't.

"Jackson."

She did.

"Really?" Troy asked. He had finished his salad and leaned back in his seat. "Do tell, Malina."

"Don't tell, Malina," I said.

She ignored me.

"There was this one time—"

"I'd been drinking," I said. Tequila. A whole lot of tequila at our end-of-season party last year. I didn't remember much, but somehow I'd been smart enough to call Malina to come get me. Not smart enough to avoid a gymnastics routine, though.

"Let the woman tell the story," Troy said, leaning toward her.

"He called me to come get him from this party. When I got there, he was the only non-passed-out one in the basement. Apparently he'd been passing the time waiting for me to arrive by going through a bin of old toys, and there happened to be one of those ribbon wands. You know, the pink, sparkly ones?"

"Oh. My. Gosh," Krista said, wide smile on her face.

As much as I wanted to shut Malina up, to remind her that she *promised* me that video would never see the light of day or even be mentioned ever again, if I said something then, I'd seem like an ass. Someone who could dish it out, but couldn't take it. So I grit my teeth and let her continue.

"Not only did he demand for me to watch while he did his routine for me, but he also demanded that I record it."

"Oh, no way," Troy said. "There's video evidence of this? I must see it. Immediately."

"It's on my old phone," Malina said. "I never uploaded it to the cloud."

Relief flooded my veins. Thank. God.

"You're safe today, Jackson," Troy said. "But the next time there's alcohol around, I can't guarantee there won't be a ribbon."

"Gee, thanks," I said, shooting daggers at Malina.

She only looked guilty for a second before smiling and turning back to Troy.

The evening continued like that. Sure, some conversations were fine, but more often than not, Malina took a jab at me, or I took one at her, or we ended up arguing over things we had absolutely no reason to argue about. When we got in an argument about whether NTDP's colors should change from red, white, and blue, I knew I was out of hand, but that didn't mean I could stop myself.

Troy and Krista started picking up on it, trying to direct the conversation to other topics, but I couldn't help it. Every time Troy flirted with Malina or casually touched her arm or made her laugh, my blood pressure rose.

But wait. I knew why *I* was freaking out on her, but why was *she* freaking out on me? Wondering about that made it even harder for me to stop.

"Well, I think we're about done here, don't you guys?" Troy asked after we'd paid our bills and Malina had made another jab at me, this one suggesting that I wouldn't be able to remember Krista's name since I'd already dated Kristy and Kristie. What was *up* with her tonight?

"Yeah. More than done," I said, taking the napkin off my lap and putting it on the table.

I wasn't positive, but I thought I heard a, "Finally," from Krista as we got up.

Normally, I'd walk next to my date, maybe take her arm or put a hand on the small of her back, but I was fuming too much for that. I walked alone. At least I held the front door for Krista when we got there. But I let it close on Troy and Malina.

"Thanks, man," Troy said sarcastically.

When we got in the car, I forced myself to calm down and drive carefully. It was mostly silent, with just Troy or Krista occasionally commenting on the song on the radio or something we drove by. I drove to Krista's house first. As we approached, I felt guilty. I hadn't really been thinking about the date from her point of view, and when I did, it wasn't pretty. When I pulled into her driveway, I left the car running but got out and walked her to her front door.

"This was—"

Krista held up a hand to stop me. "You like her."

It wasn't a question, so I didn't answer.

"You like her and didn't want her to go out with Troy alone, so you used me to get in on the date."

Guilt made me want to squirm right out of my skin. I scratched the top of my head. "When you say it like that, it makes me feel like shit."

"Good," Krista said, but then she smiled and squeezed my arm. "Talk to her. Tell her how you feel."

It wasn't that easy. Krista didn't know the background, the history, or the obstacles standing in front of us.

I sighed. "I'm really sorry. For using you. That you had to spend the evening watching the two of us fight. I didn't think…"

"That's the thing when it comes to love. You *shouldn't* think." She shrugged. "Besides, I got a good meal out of it. And I think you're going to owe me a favor sometime in the future."

I smiled and stuck my hands in my pockets. "You want NTDP tickets? You got 'em."

She laughed. "I was thinking more along the lines of you

washing my car or getting me out of a date I don't want to be on or being my DD some night so I don't have to worry about it. Or maybe all three."

I laughed. "Fair. Thanks for going with me."

"Let's not do it again sometime," she said.

"Agreed."

Someone beeped the car horn, and I flinched. I had a feeling I knew which one of the two in the car had done it.

"Talk to her," Krista said again. "Apologize for the idiotic behavior that earned you that horn honk, and then tell her how you feel."

"Thanks, Krista. Good night."

"Good night, Jackson."

The second I climbed back into the car, Troy pointed at the backseat toward Malina. "She did it."

"I know she did," I grumbled under my breath. Then instead of turning in the direction of Malina's house, I turned toward mine.

"Wait, where are we going?" Malina asked.

"I'm dropping Troy off at my house so he can get his car. Then I'll take you home."

"But my house is practically on the way," she said.

"I know."

"Wait," Troy said. "You're dropping me off first? And then you two are going to be in the car together, alone? Should I be concerned that one of you is going to end the night dead and the other's going to end the night as a murderer?"

"No murder," I said. "We just need to talk." Maybe not in the way Krista wanted us to talk, but we did need to talk. Malina and I had been best friends for too long to let tonight go. Even if nothing ever came of us, I didn't want to leave anything as messy as it was right then. "You know, unless you want us to go ahead and talk now, while you're in the car."

"No," Troy said quickly. "No. That's okay. Take me to your

house. Please. I'm good with that."

"Thought so," I said.

"I don't want to talk to you when you're being an asshole," Malina said. "Take me home."

"Oh, *I'm* the one being an asshole? What about you?"

"Hey," Troy said, holding up a hand. "I think everyone who was on this date can agree that you're both being assholes, and I think everyone in the world can agree that you should wait until I'm out of the car to talk about it."

"Fine," Malina said.

In the rearview mirror, I saw her slump down farther into her seat. Troy turned the radio up too loud to allow any of us to talk anymore. When we reached my house, where his car was parked in the street, he practically jumped out of the car.

"Thanks for dinner, Troy," Malina said.

I knew her voice well enough to know that she was feeling some of the same guilt I'd felt when I'd dropped off Krista.

"You're welcome. No murder," he said, pointing at both of us before closing the door and running to his own car.

As much as I wanted to start talking then and there, that wasn't a good decision. If things got tense, which they no doubt would, I'd still have to drive her home. Better to drive her home first, where we could duke it out and then she could go inside and I could cool off on the drive home. While I headed in the direction of the Hall household, I thought about the other times we'd fought, which weren't many.

Our biggest fight was during our sophomore year. Malina had planned her birthday party for Valentine's Day, which happened to be on a Saturday that year. Of course I wanted to be at my best friend's party, but I'd also started dating this girl who really wanted me to take her out. I'd tried to find a way to do both, but in the meantime Malina found out and freaked out. She said I was putting a girl I'd been dating for two weeks before our years of friendship. In retrospect, she was right, but at the time I was thinking with my hormones, and Malina's anger pissed me off. We yelled at each other, I missed her party, and I ended up breaking up with the girl a week later. I made it up to Malina with an apology and a slice of her favorite red velvet cheesecake. Our friendship returned to normal, but it was proof that we did know how to fight. I wasn't sure we'd bounce back from this one so quickly.

When we pulled into the Halls' driveway, I put the car in park, killed the engine, and stared hard out the windshield.

"What the *hell*, Jackson?" Malina's words shook with barely contained anger. "What is wrong with you?"

That sent my anger up a notch or seven. "Me?" I asked, spinning in my seat so I could look back at her. The only light came from a single, dim bulb on the porch, so I couldn't make out her expression, but I could imagine it. "What the hell is wrong with *you*?"

"Oh, Canada's more beautiful than Hawaii, Malina," she said, doing a terrible impression of what I'd said at dinner. "USA Hockey's colors should be friggin' green and yellow. Seriously? You weren't even making any sense tonight, and the things you brought up—"

"Me?" I asked again, incredulous. "The things *I* brought up? What about the drunk video that you *swore* would never be mentioned?"

"I only brought that up because you brought up the stomach flu incident from freshman year! Were you *trying* to embarrass me in front of Troy?"

"Yeah, well what about what you said about Krista? Did you *have* to make fun of that yearbook picture? You know she had no control over that. And why were you going after her, anyway?"

Malina leaned forward into a swath of porch light, and I hated that even with anger and frustration boiling in my blood, she was still so damn pretty.

"What about Troy?" she asked. "He's your *teammate*. Yet you basically called out the small size of his junk while he was on a date with a new girl. With *me*."

"Exactly!" I yelled. The second the word was out of my mouth, I wanted to take it back.

"Exactly *what*?" Malina asked. "Was it a problem for you that he was on a date with me? With you? Because if I remember correctly, I didn't invite you along in the first place."

"No. It's just…" I was still yelling, but I didn't know what to yell about.

"Just what?" Malina yelled back.

Krista's advice echoed through my mind. *Tell her how you feel.*

"I don't want you to date him, okay?"

She scoffed. "Yeah. Like you have any say in who *I* date, Mr. Player. Okay. Let's hear it. Why don't you want me to date Troy?"

The truth came out before I could stop it. "Because I like you, okay?"

"What?" Malina demanded, as if she hadn't heard me right.

My cheeks warmed. "Because I like you. Me. *I* like you. I don't want you to go out with him because I want you to go out with me." I braced myself for her reaction. For laughing. For pity. For her to run far, far away. Instead, I got more yelling.

"Yeah, well I like you, too!"

Everything stopped. My brain. My heart. My lungs. Cause of death: shock. "*What?*"

"I like you! Why do you think I said all of those things about you and Krista at dinner? You know I'm not a jerk! You know I wouldn't do that out of revenge for everything you were saying! It's because I like you and I didn't want to see you with her!" She huffed in frustration. "God, every time you put your hand on her arm…"

"I wanted to be putting my hand on you instead!"

"Well I didn't know that!"

"Well now you do!"

"Fine!"

"Fine!"

Just like that, with my heart threatening to explode with anger and frustration and surprise and some of the most intense desire I'd ever felt in my life, I lunged over the center console and kissed her. Hard. Not like that first kiss. Not something she could see as an accident. Not something I had to or wanted to apologize for, but a real, lip-crushing, soul-melting, heart-bursting, *desperate* kiss. And she kissed me back just as desperately.

Until she pulled away.

"Wait," she said, breathless. "This isn't right."

My heart sank. Not this. Not again. We couldn't go back to friends and pretend this didn't happen. Not now.

"Get out of the car," she said.

She got out, and I followed suit. Then she stormed around the clicking, still-cooling engine and threw herself at me so hard I fell back against the car before catching her and kissing her like I wanted to all along. Our mouths fit together perfectly. Every time I tipped my head, she met me there, stealing the breath from my lungs and making my legs go weak. I didn't know how long it'd take to make up for the years I could have been kissing her like this and hadn't, but I was determined to try.

Heat rushed to every inch of my skin that came in contact with her. I pulled her close, hands cupping her face, sliding around into her thick hair. With each touch, I understood why Malina liked astronomy so much: I saw stars. Constellations. Galaxies. And they were incredible. When I parted her lips with mine and she gasped, then moaned, I felt it all the way down to my toes. *Finally*. Even though I didn't realize it, this kiss was what I'd been waiting for, what I'd been searching for, and it had been worth the wait.

When my brain caught up to my body, I pulled back, breathing hard. "No more dating my friends. Only *me*." I didn't mean to yell, but emotions were still running too high. It was like the anger and ecstasy wires in my brain were all tangled up.

"Fine! No more dating anyone else besides *me*."

"Fine."

Then we kissed again—quick, yet fierce, sending stars shooting across the backs of my eyelids one more time—before she stormed off to the front door and I got back in the car. I slammed the door and tried to breathe. Then I started laughing and laughed until there were tears in my eyes.

I'd kissed Malina. Intentionally. Because I liked her and she liked me back. And it was the best damn kiss I'd ever had.

Why hadn't I done that in the first place?

Chapter Fifteen

MALINA

I slammed the front door and immediately started pacing the length of the entryway rug. My lips were still tingling. I could still feel the warmth of his hand on the back of my neck. Holy crap. I'd kissed Jackson. On purpose. There was no going back, which was good because I didn't want to go back. Ever.

"Hey, Lina," Mom said as I walked into the living room. She frowned as she studied me. "Everything okay?"

It was only then that I realized I had slammed the door hard enough to rattle the mirror on the wall. "Yeah," I said. "Cold out there."

She nodded and glanced up at the clock. "I didn't expect you this early."

The date had been short. It probably hadn't *felt* very short to Krista or Troy, though. Oops. "Yeah," I said. I took off my shoes and put them in their place in the closet. I wanted to head upstairs. To FaceTime Izzy and tell her what had happened. To text Jackson and say...what did you say to your best friend when you just shared the best kiss you'd had in your entire life? I didn't know, but I was willing to figure it out.

But Mom muted the TV and looked up at me with this hopeful expression like she wanted nothing more than some girl talk and asked, "So, how was it?"

I had no clue how to answer that question, either. The date itself? Pretty terrible. The unexpected detour after the date? Pretty amazing. Tutu was sitting on the couch, weaving *lauhala*. Whatever she was weaving was so early into the process that I couldn't tell what it was going to be yet. Maybe she couldn't tell, either. I forced myself to calm down and took a seat next to her, careful not to disrupt the neat pile of leaves next to her leg. "It was fine." I guessed if you took the awkward parts of the date and the incredible kiss and mashed them together, it probably evened out to "fine."

"Only fine?" Mom asked. "Was he nice?"

Troy had, in fact, been very nice. Nicer than most guys would have been if they had to put up with what Jackson and I put him through. "Very nice," I said. "Troy is a good guy."

Mom frowned and picked up a glass of water from the coaster on the end table. "You don't like him," she said before taking a sip.

It wasn't that I wanted to hide the kiss with Jackson from Mom and Tutu. It was that I wasn't sure how I was supposed to feel about it yet, so it wasn't something I was excited to talk about with adults. "I'm not sure," I said, even though I was sure. I didn't like Troy. Jackson had proved that.

Mom clucked her tongue. "Sorry, hon. First dates can be rough, though. Maybe give him another chance? Did I ever tell you about my first date with your dad?"

She had told me, probably about a hundred times. They were at the university, and neither of them had enough money to do something off-campus, so they went to some theater production. It was so boring that they both fell asleep. Mom loved telling the story, dramatizing exactly how terrible the play had been. Neither one of them knew if it was solely the production or the chemistry between them that was terrible, but when she woke up with her head on his shoulder, she knew her subconscious was telling her to give him another chance. And there they were, all those years later, still married. Still in love.

Not only had I heard the story, but I could practically tell it myself. Thankfully, the oven timer buzzed in the kitchen.

"The cookies!" Mom set her mug down. "Hold that thought. I'll be back."

"You're making cookies?" I asked. It was only then that I noticed the sugary-sweet smell wafting in from the kitchen. It had been so long since Mom had made her coconut shortbread cookies.

She smiled at me on her way to the kitchen. "You were on a date and your dad's out with the guys, so Tutu and I needed something fun to do after her appointment. I'll bring you both some."

"Deal," I said. Talking to Izzy and Jackson could wait a few minutes. After all, the date hadn't gone well enough to warrant dessert at the restaurant. "What are you making, Tutu?" I asked.

"A basket, I think," Tutu said.

It didn't look anything like a basket yet, but I believed her. I watched her hands move, shaky and slow but confident, and listened to the faint sound of Mom humming while she removed cookies from the oven.

"Malina," Tutu said, not looking up from her weaving.

"Yes?"

"You said the date was 'fine,' but you have that look."

I forced a smile and tried to hide any "look" off my face. "What look?"

"The look like you kissed a boy," Tutu said.

My cheeks flushed and I wiped at my mouth, like I could wipe away any visible evidence.

Tutu laughed. "You did kiss a boy?"

Then I felt like an idiot. I didn't have any look on my face; she was just waiting to see what my reaction would be so she'd know what I had or hadn't done. Tutu might have been old, but she was sharp. Sharper than I gave her credit for.

"Yeah," I said. Then I quickly added, "Don't tell Dad. Or Mom. Because she'll tell Dad."

Tutu waved off my concerns. "Your secret is safe. But you don't seem happy about the kiss. It wasn't good?" She glanced up from her weaving. "Did he do something you didn't want?"

There was an edge to her tone that let me know she'd be more than willing to protect me if needed. But I didn't want her thinking negatively about Troy, and certainly not about Jackson.

"No," I said. "No. Nothing like that."

This should have been awkward, talking to my grandma about this, but it wasn't really. It kind of felt like talking to a friend.

"Then what's the problem?" Tutu asked.

I sighed and picked up one of the *lauhala* leaves, running it between my fingers. "The kiss was good. It just wasn't with Troy."

Tutu looked up from her weaving and didn't return to it. She studied me for a minute, then nodded. "Jackson."

I had to fight back a smile, because oh yeah, *I'd kissed Jackson.* "Yeah. Jackson." I told her the quick version about how dinner had gone so terribly, with the jabs and anger that I'd since realized were mostly jealousy, and how we were yelling at each other in the car, and apparently the line between anger and kissing was very, very thin. And possibly dashed.

"I always liked that boy," Tutu said.

"Me, too."

She held up one finger. "But if he hurts you, I won't like him anymore."

I laughed. "Fair enough." But I couldn't think about Jackson hurting me. I could barely comprehend the beginning of this change from friends to more, let alone the end of it.

"I made something for you," Tutu said, setting aside the potential basket and reaching over to the end table.

"You did? Tutu, you didn't have to do that."

She waved off my comment and slipped a bracelet over my hand and onto my wrist. It was some of the most delicate *lauhala* weaving I'd ever seen—thin and tight and perfect.

"It's beautiful," I said. "You really made this?"

"I really did," she said. "No matter which boy is kissing you, you are beautiful and perfect exactly the way you are."

My heart melted into a pile of goo. I leaned forward and kissed her forehead. "Thank you, Tutu. So much."

"Oh, did you give it to her?" Mom asked, returning to the living room, hands completely full with a plate of cookies and three glasses of milk.

I helped her set down the snack and then held out my wrist for her to see.

"It fits perfectly. I knew it would. It's beautiful, Mom. Really beautiful."

"A beautiful bracelet for a beautiful girl." Tutu winked at me before biting into a shortbread cookie.

My secret was safe with her.

A little while later, I doubted my secret's safety with Izzy when I told her what happened with Jackson and she flipped the eff out.

"You did *what*?" she yelled.

I rolled over on my bed, farther away from the door, and turned the volume down a couple of notches so my parents wouldn't hear. "I kissed Jackson."

"Holy shit, Malina! What about Troy? What is happening? This is the last time I let you go on a double date without me, woman."

"It happened after the date, if that makes you feel any better. And as for me and Troy…we didn't quite hit it off."

"I'd hope not since you kissed Jackson!"

From the FaceTime screen, I saw her flop down onto her bed. One of her ear buds came out with the motion, but she stuck it back in.

"So, what now?" she asked. "Are you, like, dating Jackson?"

"I don't know. We didn't really talk about it. We kind of left still yelling at each other."

"Kinky?"

I rolled my eyes. "No. I…I don't know. I have no idea what's going to happen, but I'm kind of okay with that."

"Really?"

It was a fair question. For the handful of guys I'd dated in the past, I had to know where everything was going at all times. Probably drove the guys crazy. Probably was the reason I wasn't with any of them anymore, actually. But with Jackson, I wasn't in any hurry to define anything. Either we'd be a couple or we wouldn't. It felt like fate, like nothing I could control or put pressure or a timeline on. I was along for the ride. "Really," I said. "We'll see."

"We'll see," Izzy echoed.

"So how was *your* night?" I asked.

"Not nearly as exciting as yours. Babysitting and scholarship applications, mostly."

Guilt stabbed at me a little bit. I'd taken too many nights off since Jackson got home. I was behind where I needed to be, but I could catch up. I *had* to. "Yeah. I should probably go work on those for a while before bed, too."

At that second, a text message appeared on the screen above Izzy's head. I couldn't see the message of the text, but could see that it was from Jackson. My breath caught in my lungs. My heart rate practically doubled. What if he changed his mind and didn't want to be more than friends? Or what if he wanted to come over right then and become even *more* not friends?

"Hey," Izzy said, waving a hand to draw my attention back down to her. "What just happened?"

"Sorry," I said, dismissing the text with a swipe of my finger. "Jackson texted me."

"Oooh, a booty text," Izzy said, waggling her eyebrows.

"Gross, Iz," I said.

She laughed. "Okay, I should let you go respond to him."

"Okay," I said. "Thanks for listening."

"Thanks for providing some drama and entertainment to break up the scholarship monotony." She paused. "Hey, Malina?"

"Yeah?"

"You look happy."

I smiled. "I am happy. I think."

"Good," Izzy said. "Keep it that way."

"I'll do my best."

We ended the FaceTime call, and I took a breath before tapping over to my text messages.

Jackson: *I had no idea that was the way the date was going to end...but I'm really glad it did.*

If he hadn't been my best friend before this, I might have thought it was corny. Cheesy. But he *was* my best friend. And I knew he was telling the truth.

Me: *Me too.*

Then I fell back onto my bed with my phone clutched to my chest, smiling so wide my face hurt.

The scholarships could wait a few more minutes.

Chapter Sixteen

JACKSON

I'd been home from the disaster of a date for less than an hour. Well, the date had been a disaster, but what had happened after the date hadn't been a disaster at all. While sitting on the edge of my bed, I'd composed no fewer than ten text messages to Troy, but this wasn't an easy text to send. Not only did I have to apologize for my shitty behavior during the date, but I also had to tell him what happened after the date. That I liked Malina. Plus, I had to say all of that in a way that would allow us to keep working well together on the team and hopefully keep him from slitting my throat with a hockey skate.

But while my thumbs were hovering over the screen, typing and then erasing over and over again, a message came through.

Troy: *Dude, why didn't you tell me you like Malina?*

My cheeks warmed, and I winced.

Me: *That obvious?*

Troy: *I knew she was your best friend. Didn't know you were into her until tonight, but yeah. Pretty obvious.*

Me: *Sorry for being an ass.*

Troy: *Don't worry about it.*

Troy: *Hey, you don't actually have a thing for Krista, do you?*

Though I'd spent most of the date focused on Malina, I did have a vague recollection of Troy and Krista talking while Malina and I were arguing. I'd thought it had been their way of dealing with the awkwardness Malina and I had created, but maybe there was something more there.

Me: *No.*

Me: *Why, are you into her?*

Troy: *Maybe. I got her number while you and Malina were arguing. I might ask her out.*

Troy: *And sorry, dude, but you are NOT invited.*

I literally laughed out loud.

Me: *Fair. Thanks, man.*

Troy: *See you at practice tomorrow.*

Before I could set my phone down, another text came through. I expected it to be Troy, saying something about how he'd be glad Coach was back so Pierce wouldn't be in charge and kill us all again, but it wasn't from him.

Krista: *Did you kiss her?*

I couldn't help but smile as my thumbs hovered over the keyboard.

Me: *Yes.*

Krista: *:)*

Krista: *Good. I would've kicked your ass if you didn't.*

Me: *Sorry again.*

Krista: *Don't worry about it. Everyone in that restaurant knew you two belong together...except you two. Now you know.*

Me: *Now we know.*

After saying good night to Krista (who I really hoped would end up with Troy, not only because it would make me feel a little less guilty, but because they were both nice people), I stretched out against my pillows and checked my Snapchats. There was a ridiculous one from Pierce. The filter made him look like a baby and turned his voice ridiculously high pitched.

"Hey, Jackson," he said. Then, "Lia, look how adorable I am. Don't you want to say hi to Jackson?"

Normal Lia appeared on the screen for a second before the filter found her face and transformed her into baby Lia. She somehow looked even more ridiculous than Pierce. The message cut off while the two of them were still cracking up. It almost made me want to forgive him for the terrible practice.

Almost.

I made it through all of my messages and my Instagram feed, but I still wasn't tired. I clicked over to the NTDP forums. Usually, I was good about responding to fans and answering questions, but I'd been slacking since I got home.

Since Malina. One fan who posted regularly to the forums commented on the fact that I was MIA. I quickly thumbed out an apology and responded to a few more posts. Scouts could look at the forums as easily as fans could. The last thing I wanted was a scout thinking I wasn't completely dedicated to hockey, even if I did have a few distractions right then. Or one big distraction.

After I crawled between the sheets and shut off the light, my brain still wouldn't quit. I rolled over and grabbed my phone again. Texting Malina shouldn't have felt weird. I shouldn't have felt nervous. It did, and I was, but I hit send anyway.

Me: *Hey*

It took less than a minute for her to respond. Maybe I wasn't the only one who was having trouble sleeping.

Malina: *Hey :)*

Malina: *What's up?*

Just seeing texts from her made me so energetically happy, I wasn't sure I'd ever sleep again.

Me: *Can't sleep.*

She sent the shocked-face emoji and immediately started typing again.

Malina: *You can't sleep? But sleeping is your second best talent besides hockey! I heard that you once slept through fireworks on the Fourth of July.*

Me: *Cut me a break, I was like five.*

Malina: *Fine. So why can't you sleep tonight?*

A cheesy response entered my brain—"Because I was thinking about a completely different kind of fireworks! ;)"—but I resisted the urge to type it. Maybe that was something I would say to another girl, and I *had* said many similar things over the years, but this was Malina. Before I could figure out what I *should* say, she started typing again.

Malina: *Wait, is it kiss fireworks that's keeping you up this time?*

I grinned and shook my head. The girl knew me too well. Maybe that was the best part about dating your best friend.

Me: *You got it.*

Me: *Can't stop thinking about you in general, but especially can't stop thinking about that kiss.*

Me: *We should have done that a long time ago.*

Malina: *No, because then we wouldn't have been best friends all those years. Then it might have been just a kiss, not a kiss with fireworks. Maybe we needed those years.*

Considering the fact that I already felt differently about her than I'd felt about the many other girls I'd dated, maybe she was right.

When I finally fell asleep, it was with a smile on my face and my phone in my hand.

Chapter Seventeen

MALINA

I was digging through my locker when I felt someone come up behind me. I glanced over my shoulder and did this kind of melty thing that I wasn't entirely proud of and probably couldn't quite hide. How had I ignored my feelings for Jackson? How did I let girl after girl kiss him without realizing that *I* was the one who should be kissing him?

"Hey," I said.

"Hey."

"Can I…" He hesitated. "Can I kiss you?"

The fact that awkwardness was radiating off him in waves was kind of cute. Instead of answering, I leaned in and kissed him. Goose bumps immediately formed on my skin for reasons that had nothing to do with the temperature of the school hallway. The kiss might not have been a surprise or out of anger, but it still felt *right*. The awkwardness melted away when his lips pressed against mine, soft and sure. He tasted sweet, like mint toothpaste and everything that was good in the world.

When we pulled apart, I smiled. "Are you going to ask my permission every time you want to kiss me?"

"Sorry," he said, looking down at the ground. "It's different. Between us. You know? Because—"

"I know this is a little weird," I said, "but I'll save you the trouble. The answer will always be 'yes.'"

He smiled and leaned in to kiss me again, this time without asking.

A sudden voice behind us made both of us jump and pull apart.

"What the fuck am I looking at? My eyes! My eyes!"

Relief washed over me when I realized who it was. "Izzy," I said, exasperated. "Why would you do that?"

She was wearing leggings, a hugely oversize sweater, and the biggest shit-eating grin I'd ever seen on her face.

"Because I can," she said.

"Nice," Jackson said with an eye roll.

Izzy stood to her full height and turned to Jackson, arms folded across her chest. "You. What exactly are your intentions with my best friend?"

"To make her fall in love with me, knock her up, give her an STD, and then break her heart," he deadpanned.

"Jackson," I said, poking his side. "Don't."

Izzy held up two fists. "I will beat you up."

"I believe you," he said. Then he put an arm around my shoulders. "But you won't need to, because my intentions are exactly the opposite of everything I just said. Except maybe the 'love' thing."

Even though we were far from saying we loved each other, even hearing him say the word made my heart swell with hope for the future. I leaned into him. It felt so nice being at Jackson's side. It felt nice *belonging* at Jackson's side.

"Good," Izzy said. Then she grinned. "It's about damn

time, you two."

"Sorry, but we were busy being friends," I said.

Izzy rolled her eyes. "You and I both know a guy and a girl can't be friends unless one or more is gay."

"Hey, we were just friends since elementary school," Jackson said.

"Yeah, and look at you now. Sucking face. Burning my retinas."

"What," Jackson said, "you mean like this?"

He used one finger to tip my chin up. I let my eyes fall shut right before he kissed me, soft and sweet and making me wonder again why we'd waited all those years to do this.

"Come *on*," Izzy said with a moan. "Get a room."

Jackson smiled against my lips before pulling away. He was still smiling when I opened my eyes and looked up at him.

"Sorry, Iz," I said. "It's his fault."

"I know it is, and I don't forgive him. But I do get to leave because I have an appointment with Mrs. Braxton. That woman gave me a B+ on my last Shakespeare paper."

I grabbed the last book I would need out of my locker and closed the door. "A B+ is good, isn't it?"

"No. It's scholarship season. A B+ is terrible."

Jackson leaned against my closed locker door. "Wait, I'm in that class with you. Aren't you the one who bragged that you didn't even read *Hamlet*?"

Izzy scuffed one foot against the floor. "Well, yes, but that doesn't matter. I did some damn good writing in that paper. Should have been an A- at least. Wish me luck."

"Good luck," I said. As she walked away, I said, "And read the book next time."

She didn't even bother turning around as she waved me off. Sometimes the girl was too smart for her own good.

I leaned against the locker next to Jackson. He intertwined my fingers with his. One of our classmates shot us a dirty look as she walked by. My stomach flipped. I couldn't remember the girl's name, but I did remember that Jackson had dated her. Was that the end of last year or the beginning of this year? It might have been the first dirty look I'd gotten from one of Jackson's exes, but I knew it wouldn't be the last. It was something I was going to have to deal with.

He toyed with the new bracelet on my wrist. "This is pretty," he said. "Very Hawaiian."

"Isn't it great? Tutu weaved it for me."

"She's amazing."

"She definitely is." I toyed with the bracelet for another second before letting my arm drop. "So, what are you doing tonight?" I asked. "Want to hang out? I think we need to go on a date where we don't yell terrible things at each other."

He laughed. "We do. Unfortunately, it's a Terrible Trio night."

"Terrible Trio" was the name Jackson had given to the marathon hockey nights where the guys started with off-ice conditioning, took a break for food and a boring team meeting, and then went to on-ice practice. They didn't happen often, but he wasn't a fan of them when they did.

"What time will you be done?" I asked.

"Nine," he said. "But honestly, by the time I shower and eat, I'll be ready to collapse for the night." He squeezed my hand. "Sorry."

My heart sank. I hoped my disappointment didn't show on my face. "That's fine," I said, forcing myself to believe the words. "I have a ton of homework and scholarship work to do anyway."

"What are you doing tomorrow night?" he asked. "I have practice, but it only goes until seven."

I consulted my mental calendar. "I have a STEM meeting that starts at seven," I said.

He grinned a little. "You know, I think we're going to be

really good at this 'dating' thing."

I elbowed him playfully in the ribs. "Stop. We'll be great. We can go out this weekend, right?" I'd planned to spend all weekend working, and I had my scholarship interview, but surely I'd be able to find a couple of hours to spend with Jackson. I'd *make* a couple of hours to spend with Jackson.

"Yeah," he said. "I have a home game Friday night. Will you be there?"

"Sure," I said. At the beginning of the season, it wasn't much fun to go to Jackson's games. They'd lost over and over again, mostly due to Pierce's struggles. But he'd turned around whatever the problem was, and they were on a winning streak. Hopefully I wouldn't have to watch this game from between my fingers.

"Good. Because I need you in the stands to cheer me on. And we'll find a time to go on a real date. I promise."

"I believe you," I said.

Then he grinned at me. Just stood there and grinned.

A self-conscious feeling made me run my tongue along my teeth, as if I'd missed a giant piece of spinach when I brushed them this morning. "What?"

"This," he said, with a little shake of his head.

"What?" I asked again, still not getting it.

"You. Me. This." He leaned down and kissed me, short but sweet. "I'm happy. Are you happy?"

If the way the force of gravity suddenly seemed a lot less than normal wasn't happiness, I didn't know what was. "Very," I said, and kissed him again.

"Remember, juniors and seniors, you can enter one project into the scholarship competition. However, a win in one of the categories does not guarantee a scholarship win, and a scholarship win does not guarantee a win in one of the categories." Mr. Palmer was one of those teachers who made you appreciate natural speaking voices—ones with inflection, animation, enthusiasm—simply because he didn't have any of those things. As the STEM coordinator, he was definitely part of the T, which meant he spent more time with technology than he did with other people. That was saying something, considering he spent much of his time interacting with students.

"Any questions about the scholarship part of the competition?"

I raised my hand.

Mr. Palmer nodded at me. "Yes…Miss…"

It wasn't any surprise that, even though this was my fourth year involved in the STEM program, Mr. Palmer couldn't remember my name. It definitely wasn't personal. The guy couldn't remember to trim his nose or ear hairs, let alone remember any of our names. Though I wasn't in any of his classes, I assumed he gave everyone an A simply because he couldn't tell students apart.

"It's more of a general question," I said. "Is that okay?"

He motioned for me to continue.

"Do our projects have to be completely finalized by next week?"

"Yes. You may still make minor tweaks up until the day of the competition, but the vast majority of the project must be complete so we can determine which projects will be selected in each category."

I wasn't so much worried about the "will my project be selected" thing. My project could fit into many different categories, and seniors' projects tended to be the first picks. Plus, my project should be impressive. If I could get it working. That was the part that had me worried.

Ever since that first, accidental kiss, I'd been spending

too much time thinking about Jackson. Wasting hours that I really should have spent working on the project. Working on scholarship applications. I'd read an article recently that broke down different jobs and loans and found that without scholarships, most people were financially better off not going to college than going and being unable to pay loans. The job with my dad's car company? It would barely be enough to pay off loans. Barely. But at least I'd have one foot in the door. Most college graduates didn't even have that.

"Miss...?" Mr. Palmer said, interrupting my thoughts.

I jolted. The meeting was over. Most of my classmates were gone, and the last few were packing up their things.

"Sorry," I said, immediately closing my notebook and shoving it into my bag.

"It's okay," Mr. Palmer said. He studied me. "Are you still working on the scientifically accurate light-reflecting solar system controlled by the app?"

Go figure. The guy couldn't remember my one syllable last name, but he could remember exactly what I'd been working on for the last year. "Yes," I said.

His face lit up. "Good. I can't wait to see it."

Yeah, I thought.

You and me both.

Chapter Eighteen

"Ta-da," I said as I flipped on the basement light.

"I've definitely never been in your basement," Malina said.

"That's because the only thing that's down here is my workout equipment." I motioned to the weights and the treadmill I used when the Michigan weather was too intense for running outside, which was most of the year. "Well, my workout equipment and this card table, which I set up for you." Malina and I wanted to see each other, but were also both dealing with pressure. I had hockey pressure, and she had school/college/scholarship pressure. Our compromise was that she would come over and work on stuff while I worked out. We'd get to be together, and when we both finished, we'd hang out as our reward.

"It's perfect," she said, setting her backpack on the table and taking her laptop out.

While she waited for it to boot up, she crossed her arms

over her chest and shivered. The basement was unfinished, so it was pretty cold down there. I'd warm up as soon as I started working out, but I'd already thought of a solution for her. I grabbed the sweatshirt I'd draped over the chair and held it out to her.

She smiled. "So sweet. Thank you."

"You're welcome."

When she pulled it over her head, she was still smiling. "It smells like you."

"Yeah?" I asked. "Is that a good thing?" Then I pulled her toward me. She might have been focused on how the sweatshirt smelled, but I was more focused on how she looked wearing it. Seriously hot.

"A very good thing," she said.

The sleeves were too long for her, so I rolled them up past her wrists. Then I took her hands in mine, intertwining my fingers with hers, and kissed her. I wanted more, so I put my hands on the small of her back and pulled her close, kissing down her neck to the spot where my sweatshirt met her skin.

"Hey," she said softly, pulling away a little.

"What?" I asked in between kisses.

"You're supposed to be working out."

With a grin, I took two of her fingers and pushed them against the pulse point in my neck. "I *am* working out."

She raised an eyebrow. "Oh, this is one of your coach's approved workouts?"

"It should be. I'll submit it to him for his approval." I leaned in and kissed her on the lips again, tasting her smile.

She let me go on for another few seconds, then pulled back. "Hey," she said. "You might be getting a workout, but I'm definitely not getting any work done. I have that paper due on Monday, and I'm barely even through the outline. Plus there are two more scholarship application deadlines next week. And then I—"

"Okay, okay," I said, forcing myself to step back. "I get it. I'm distracting you." I took another step back. "I'll be over here. Working out. And you'll be over there. Doing smart people things."

"Right." She sat down at the table, took a notebook and pen out of her bag, and started working.

Meanwhile, I jumped on the treadmill. My usual routine was to jog a mile or two to warm up and then hit the weights. It was an arm day. My legs were sore from my last leg day, but they started to loosen up as I jogged.

The good thing was that the treadmill faced away from Malina, so I couldn't be distracted by the sight of her and do something idiotic like miss a step and fall flat on my face. The bad thing was that I usually blasted music while I ran, and without that to distract me, all I could think about was her.

At one point, I glanced over my shoulder at her. It almost caused a misstep, but I caught myself at the last second. She was hard at work, her fingers flying over the keys, her forehead wrinkled in concentration. I forced myself to mentally run through some of the team's newest plays to keep my brain where it needed to be.

Once my muscles were warm, I took a drink of water and hit the weights. I started with the dumbbell bench press. The first set of reps was easy with that weight, but I knew by the third set, it would be a struggle. I sat up after the first set to give my chest and arms a little break, and glanced over at Malina. She was staring at me, but the second my eyes met hers, she startled and turned back to the computer, knocking her pen on the ground in the process.

Good to know I wasn't the only one who was distracted. "How's it going?"

"Good," she said quickly. She picked up the pen and pointedly did not look at me.

"Good." Since she was watching, and because I was warm

enough from my run to make up for the cold basement, I took off my shirt. I laid back down on the bench for my next set with my head toward her, giving her full view of my bare shoulders and chest. Once half the set was over, I let myself tip my head back and look at her. She was watching me again, pen at the corner of her mouth, but of course the second we made eye contact, she flinched.

"Stop it!" she said.

I laughed, straightened my head, and did another rep. "Stop what? I'm working out. Wasn't this the agreement?"

"Yes, but…"

I did two more reps, each one a little more challenging than the one before. "But what?"

"Never mind," she said. "I'm going back to work."

I didn't necessarily believe her, but I said, "Okay," anyway. I finished the set and sat up. When I looked over this time, she was actually working. I managed to keep my focus through the last set of reps, and the first set of tricep dips. But when I sat on the bench to rest, I found myself staring at Malina. There was something sexy about watching her work. The concentration was clear on her face. Her fingers tapped the keys with intention and purpose. Every once in a while, she'd mouth the words she was typing. I wasn't sure if she realized she was doing it. What I *was* sure about was that I loved watching her lips move.

Those lips distracted me until I noticed her fingers slowing on the keys. Finally, she looked over at me. This time, she raised both eyebrows.

"What?" I asked.

"You're not doing anything."

Oh. I guessed that particular break between sets was a little longer than normal. Okay, a lot longer than normal. "Right." I grinned, put my hands back on the bench, and dropped back into the dips. I forced myself to stay focused on counting, but Malina didn't go back to work. She stared as I lifted myself up and down, up and down. When I finished the end of the second set, I sat on the bench and gave my arms a little shake.

"Hey," I said.

She physically snapped back to attention. "What?"

"You're not doing anything," I teased.

She sighed and ran a hand through her long hair. "You're right. This was a terrible idea. We suck at staying focused."

It was true. I slid over on the bench, patted the empty space, and motioned for her to come join me. When she didn't immediately come over, I said, "Come on. You're not getting much done anyway. Come do some tricep dips with me."

"Are they hard? You know I have noodle arms."

"There's only one way to fix that."

At that, she shoved the computer aside and came to sit next to me. I showed her how to position her wrists so she wouldn't hurt them and how to dip down, focusing on keeping her elbows in instead of flailing out to the sides.

"Like this?" she asked.

I nodded. She had good form. "Like that."

"This isn't so hard," she said, picking up the pace a little.

"Talk to me when you're in your third set."

When we took a break after her first set, she rolled her wrists. "Which muscle does this work?"

"Your triceps," I said. When she didn't respond in recognition, I turned my arm and flexed it, then pointed to the correct muscle.

"Oh," she said.

Transfixed, she reached up and ran one finger along my arm, outlining the muscle. The basement-cold of her touch felt like ice against the workout-warm of my skin. Though my arms were tired from having completed my third set, I kept the muscle flexed.

"I like your tricep," she said. Then she studied her own "noodle arms." "Mine...not so much. I'm not sure I have a tricep."

With a laugh, I turned and pulled one leg over the bench so I was facing her. "Let's see," I said. Through the fabric of my sweatshirt, I ran my fingers over her thin arm until I found her tricep. "It's there," I said. "Come on. Flex it."

She frowned. "I *am* flexing it."

I gave her arm a little squeeze. "That's okay. It's perfect."

She lifted one hand to touch the front of my arm. "This is the bicep, right?"

I flexed it for her. "You got it."

She ran her fingers up my arms to the tops of my shoulders. I shivered, but whether it was due to the fact that I was shirtless and rapidly cooling down in a cold basement or from her touch was a toss-up.

"What muscles are these?" she asked. "Shoulderceps?"

I laughed. "For someone so smart, you're really not up on human anatomy, are you?"

She glanced up from my shoulders long enough to smile. "I've been much more into physical sciences than biological ones. But right now..."

I grinned at her. "I'm glad I'm having an influence on you." I motioned for her to turn and face me. She swung one leg over the bench, as well. I slid a few inches closer to her. I put my hands on her shoulders, where she'd just been touching mine. "Trapezius," I said. I let my hands drop a little lower, but not too low. "Pectorals," I said.

"Trapezius and pectorals," she echoed. "I think those might be some of my favorites."

"Yeah? You want to end the anatomy lesson there?"

She gave a firm shake of her head. "Keep going."

I slid my hands down to the sides of her rib cage. "Intercostal muscles. Those aren't very big or strong. But these…" I let my hands drop down to her sides. Then I slid my hands up her shirt to rest in the same place. I brushed my thumbs against her abs. Her skin was warm, and she shivered against my hands. I liked making Malina shiver. A lot. "These are your obliques. Big. Strong."

"Not as strong as yours," she said. Her voice was barely above a whisper.

"You don't have to be as strong as me," I said. "You're perfect the way you are."

Then I slid closer to her on the bench, closing the distance between us, and kissed her. She melted into me and kissed me back, taking some control and making my heart race faster than the treadmill had. When my sweatshirt got in the way, she pulled back long enough to let me tug it over her head. I wanted to take the other shirt with it, but I settled for letting my hands explore through the thin fabric of her shirt, taking in what my eyes couldn't.

My tongue was doing its own exploration of her mouth when a voice startled me.

"Luke!"

I bit my own tongue in surprise and pulled back, wincing at the pain. There, standing at the bottom of the stairs, was Mom. Ice cooled the heat that had been building in my veins.

"*Malina?*" Mom asked, incredulous, looking back and forth between the two of us. "What are you *doing*?"

"Ms. Reed, I'm really—"

I cut Malina off mid-apology. "Ever heard of knocking?" I asked my mom.

"You know, it's funny. Knocking isn't a requirement when you sign the mortgage documents. And it's especially not a requirement when your son is down in the basement all alone with a girl. With your shirt off, I might add."

The ridiculousness of the situation almost made me laugh. In less than a year, I'd be a professional hockey player, but I couldn't be alone with a girl in the house? But since it was Mom's house, Mom's rules, I didn't say that. Malina handed me the sweatshirt I'd pulled off her, and I put it on over my head. "I was working out." I motioned to the card table I'd set up. "Malina was working on stuff for school."

"Uh huh," Mom said. "That's exactly what it looked like you were doing." She pinched the bridge of her nose before turning to Malina. "I think you should go home."

Malina didn't waste any time. She hopped up from the bench, shut her laptop, and shoved everything back into her bag.

"Here," I said, taking it so I could carry it upstairs for her.

Mom stepped aside and motioned for us to walk up first, like if we let her go first, we'd turn around and start having sex before her feet hit the first floor. But I didn't say anything about that—just let Malina go in front of me and followed behind her, trying not to stare at her gluteus maximus too much as we went.

When we reached the top of the stairs, Malina turned to my mom. "I am really sorry, Ms. Reed. It won't happen again."

"You're right it won't," Mom said firmly. Then she turned to me. "Drive her home. I know exactly how long it takes to drive to the Halls' house. I suggest you don't stop for any yellow lights."

"Good night, Ms. Reed," Malina said.

"Good night, Malina. Tell your parents and grandma I said hello."

"I will." As soon as we were out the front door, Malina groaned. "Oh my gosh, your mom is going to kill me."

I opened the passenger door for her. Once I was in the driver's seat and pulling away from the house, I said, "No, she's not. Trust me. She'll be pissed at me for a little while, but she didn't kill any of the other girls."

"Oh, so you've had lots of girls alone down in your

basement? That 'work out' thing was practiced?"

My face warmed. I hadn't thought that one through very well. "No, no. You're the only one." I took a turn toward her house and cleared my throat. "But I have had girls other places, and…" *Shit*. That sounded worse. "I mean that—"

"Jackson," Malina said. "Relax. We're best friends. I know your dating history. It's not something you have to hide from me. And, believe it or not, I still want to do this. Still want to do us. For as long as we both want that."

Relief cooled the embarrassment that had been heating my skin. I was lucky to have this girl. I'd always been lucky to have her as a friend, but I was even luckier to have her as more than a friend. "I want that, too."

"Good. But I hoped I'd be able to stay on your mom's good side for a tiny bit longer than that, you know?"

"She'll get over it," I said. There was a traffic light in front of us, but thankfully it was green. "It was probably a shock."

Malina groaned and put her face in her hands. "I can't believe your mom walked in on us making out."

I couldn't resist a smile. "Hey, at least only one of us was shirtless."

She lightly punched my arm.

"Ow," I said. "That hurt. Have you been working on your triceps?"

She laughed. Man, I loved making the girl laugh. I pulled into her driveway.

"Thanks for the ride," she said. "Sorry you didn't get much done on your work out."

"Sorry you didn't get much done on your schoolwork. But not really." I put the car in park. "Hey, should we go make out somewhere in your house? Let your parents find us? Get both sets of parents out of the way in one evening?"

She laughed again. "No way. See, because my dad *would* kill you. We're going to have to ease into this one."

I nodded. I could picture Mr. Hall being a little protective. Okay, a *lot* protective.

"Tutu knows, though," she said.

"How?"

Malina shrugged. "She always seems to know everything that's going on with me."

"And?"

"She seemed fine with it. I wouldn't be surprised if you get extra *poi* out of the deal."

"Now that's a win-win." I leaned over the center console and kissed her, cupping one hand around the back of her neck.

She let me go for a few more seconds before pulling back. "No yellow lights, remember?"

I sighed. "No yellow lights."

We said good night, and I made sure she got into the house safely before backing out of the driveway. When I hit the stoplight at the end of the street, I called Lacey. She'd texted me earlier and asked me to call, but I'd been a terrible brother and forgotten about it until then.

"About time, little brother," Lacey said.

"I know. Sorry."

"It's echoey. Are you in the car?"

"Yeah. You're on Bluetooth while I drive home. What's up?"

"Just checking on Mom. Did she delete Tinder?"

With everything with Malina, I hadn't paid as close attention as I probably should have. "Not sure. But no creepy old guys have showed up at our front door, so I think that's a good sign."

"Definitely," she said. "Thanks for keeping an eye on her for me."

"No problem."

"So what's up with you since the last time we talked?"

I sighed. "Mom walked in on me making out with

someone."

A pause. "And? Hate to say it, but that's far from the first time that's happened, right?"

I winced. "Not someone. Malina. We were down in the basement. Alone. Making out. And I may or may not have been shirtless."

Lacey gasped. "I'm going to ignore the TMI for a second and make sure I heard you right. Malina? Malina Hall?"

"The one and only."

"Damn, little brother. It's about time. I always thought you two would end up together, like some cheesy romantic comedy."

"Yeah, yeah. Apparently everyone else thought that, too."

"Are you happy?"

"Very."

"Good. Just be careful with her."

Something about the warning made the hair on the back of my neck stand on end. "What do you mean?"

A pause. "I know your...track record with girls. And I also know that Malina isn't any girl. She's your best friend. Don't hurt her, okay?"

"I won't," I said, a little indignant. I was capable of not hurting someone. Maybe the only reason I broke up with all those other girls was because I was supposed to be with Malina all along.

"Good," Lacey said.

I pulled into the driveway and switched the phone off Bluetooth before cutting the engine.

"You home?" she asked.

"Yeah. Not really excited about going to get lectured. Or have a sex talk."

"Ew."

"Exactly. I'll keep an eye on the dating thing though, okay?"

Lacey thanked me again, and we disconnected the call. Then I took a deep breath and headed up to the house.

My goal was simple: get inside as quickly and quietly as possible, sneak up to my room, and pretend to be asleep. I opened the door and closed it soundlessly behind me. I took quick, tip-toed steps through the hall and was almost to the stairs when—

"Stop."

My heart sank. So much for that plan. I stopped.

"Turn."

I turned.

Mom was at the kitchen counter with a dry erase marker in her hand, working on what looked to be a seating arrangement for some event. Some of the names were written in blue, some were written in red, and some were written in green. I wondered what the green meant. Aliens?

"Yes?" I asked.

"Luke, what in the world were you doing with a girl in the basement?"

I assumed she didn't want the literal answer to that question. "It's not a big deal," I said. "I have Malina in my bedroom all the time. You've never cared before."

"Yeah, because you were friends before. Nothing more. From what I saw, you two are a lot more now."

Despite the fact that I was getting in trouble, I couldn't keep a small smile from my face. "Okay, so now the rules change?" I asked, deciding to play naive and praying it would work.

"The rules absolutely change. The same rules now apply to Malina that apply to any other girl. No being alone with her *anywhere* in the house."

"Fine," I said. "And so you know, nothing was going to happen."

At least I didn't *think* anything was going to happen.

"See that it doesn't," Mom said. "I'm way too young to be a grandma."

"Absolutely too young," I said, playing to her vanity. "Practically too young to be a mom. Are you sure you didn't adopt me?"

She rolled her eyes. "Flattery will get you everywhere. Hey, totally off topic, but I got an email from your guidance counselor about a college night for parents. Information about scholarships and stuff. I think I'm going to go."

I frowned. "Why would you go to that?"

"Luke," she said with a sigh, "we talked about this. You need to apply to a few schools. Just in case."

An argument bubbled up to my lips, but tonight didn't feel like the right time to have this battle—not when I was already in trouble—so I said, "Fine."

"Good. Now get out of here so I can finish this."

I saluted Mom and headed toward the stairs. My foot was on the first step when she stopped me.

"Luke?"

I paused and turned again. The green marker was uncapped in her hand.

"Yeah?"

"I like Malina. A lot."

I smiled. "Me, too."

"Be careful with her, okay?"

I rolled my eyes. First Lacey, then Mom. Did no one have faith in me? Just because I didn't *want* to stay with one girl before didn't mean I *couldn't*. "Yeah. I got it."

"Good."

It was only when I dropped onto my bed that I realized I'd barely started and definitely hadn't finished my workout. There was no doubt that I played better when I was in my best shape, which was when I was doing my own workouts in addition to ones with the team. I'd already skipped a few workouts since I'd been home. But the bed was comfortable and I was tired and all I really wanted to do was text Malina, which wouldn't be easy with weights in my hands. The weights could wait for another day.

Chapter Nineteen

Malina

When I got home from school on Friday afternoon, my mom's car was in the driveway, but the house was empty. Usually my parents told me when they weren't going to be home, so I sent a quick *"Where are you?"* text before walking over to my STEM project. I had a few hours before I had to leave for Jackson's game, and I had to make a decision. Either I could work on my project, which probably still wouldn't work by the time it was due on Monday, or I could work on my essay for school, which was also due Monday and *needed* to be done. With one last touch to the cool glass of the farthest planet from the sun—Neptune—I resigned myself to giving up. I'd gotten so close. Maybe I'd make it work that summer, when I had more time. But not then. Not with everything else I had going on.

Maybe if this thing with Jackson hadn't happened, I would have finished in time, but it was my fault for being distracted, and I had to deal with the consequences. I let Neptune go and headed to the couch to work on something that wasn't nearly as challenging or rewarding, but much more stable. That seemed to be becoming a theme in my life.

It only took a few minutes before I was completely absorbed in my work, and therefore was kind of annoyed when my cell phone rang. It was my dad. Couldn't he text me and tell me where they were instead?

"Hello?" I said, not doing a very good job of hiding the annoyance in my voice.

"Hey, Malina."

Then he hesitated.

My stomach clenched. Something wasn't right. "What's wrong?"

"Honey, I hate to have to tell you this, but Tutu had another stroke."

Numbness flashed through my limbs, making me drop the folder I'd been holding. Papers scattered in a million directions. "*What?* Is she…is…" I couldn't make myself say the words. I couldn't even *think* them.

"She's okay," he said quickly. "Or the doctors are optimistic that she will be. Your mom knew the signs as soon as she saw them and got her to the hospital right away."

Relief warmed some of the terrified chill in my body, but a lump still formed in my throat. "Where are you?" I asked. "I'm coming."

"They transferred her to Ann Arbor as soon as she was stable," he said. "She's still in ICU. Sweetheart, we don't think you should drive all the way out here. Minors aren't allowed to visit in the ICU. Plus, you have your big scholarship interview tomorrow."

"I don't care. I'll sit in the waiting room. And I'll miss the interview. I can't sit here and do nothing."

"So don't do nothing," Dad said. "Go to Jackson's game like you were supposed to. Go to the interview in the morning.

Hopefully, by tomorrow, Tutu will be out of the ICU, and you can visit her then. You know that's what she'd want."

A tear slipped down my cheek. It *was* what she'd want, but that didn't mean it was what I wanted. It also didn't mean I was any less worried.

"Malina?" Dad asked when I didn't say anything.

"Can I talk to Mom?" I choked out as another tear fell.

"Sure. Hang on."

There was a sound of shuffling, then Mom's voice came across the line.

"Lina," she said, "are you okay?"

"Is Tutu okay?" It wasn't that I didn't believe my dad; it was just that I needed to hear it twice.

"She will be. Her neurologist is taking good care of her. Everyone is. It will be an uphill climb, exactly like last time, but Tutu was strong then and will be strong now."

I nodded even though my mom couldn't see it. "Okay. I still think I should be there."

"I won't stop you if this is where you want to be, but there's not a lot we can do tonight. Tutu's resting, and she needs that more than she needs us. I'm going to find a hotel room to spend the night. Dad can come home if you want him to."

The thought of my mom having to be in a hotel room alone while worrying about Tutu was not an option. I took a deep breath. "No. That's okay. Dad can stay there. I'll be okay."

"Are you sure?" Mom asked.

"Positive. You're right. There's nothing I can do right now. I'll go to Jackson's game. I'll go to the interview. I'll get ahead on work so I'll be free to be at the hospital as soon as she *can* have visitors."

"Tutu will love that," Mom said. "We'll keep you posted, but call or text us if you need anything, okay?"

After we said good-bye and ended the call, I just stood

there. There was no way I could focus on homework then. My hands were shaking, so I wasn't even sure I could pick up the pieces of paper I'd dropped. There was only one thing I knew I could do. Had to do.

The phone rang three times, which was just long enough for me to worry he wouldn't pick up.

"Hello?"

The sound of his voice brought tears to my eyes and clogged my throat with emotion. "Jackson," I said.

"Malina? What's wrong?"

"It's Tutu. She…" My sobs got in the way of finishing the sentence.

"Tutu? Is she—" He swore under his breath. "Where are you? Are you at home?"

"Yes," I managed to say.

"I'm on my way. Be there in ten minutes, okay?"

I heard his car in my driveway in a lot less than ten minutes, which had to say something about how fast he drove on the way. When I opened the front door, he wrapped me in his arms and let me cry into his shoulder. He rubbed my back until I calmed down a little, then took my shoulders and held me out at arm's length. Concern was written all over his face.

"What happened?"

"She had another stroke," I said, "She's in the ICU. But my parents say she's going to be okay."

He swore under his breath before pulling me into his arms again. "I'm glad she's going to be okay, but still scary, yeah?"

Safely in his arms, layers of fear started to melt away. When he let go of me again, he thumbed the tears away from my eyes.

"What can I do?" he asked. "Do you need a ride to the hospital?"

It was only then that I noticed he was wearing a shirt and tie. His usually messy hair was styled, and he was wearing something other than tennis shoes or hockey skates. It was one of my favorite things about hockey—the guys got dressed up to go to the rink for a game.

"Your game," I said. "Are you going to be late?"

"Not yet, but even if I am, I can talk to Coach. What do you need me to do?"

"Take me to your game." I explained what my mom and dad had said, and that I needed distraction more than anything else tonight.

"You're sure?" he asked.

I wiped at my eyes again, took a deep breath, and nodded. "Let's go."

"Jackson, Malina," someone called from behind us as we walked up to the rink.

When I turned, I saw Lia. We slowed so she could catch up.

"Hey," she said.

"Oh, good," Jackson said, opening the door for us. "You two are both here early. You can hang out together while Pierce and I warm up with the team."

There was something about the robotic way he said it that made me suspect this wasn't a coincidence.

Once we were inside, I nodded toward her outfit, which included a U.S. Figure Skating sweatshirt, a pair of leggings, and her hair in a bun. "Did you just get out of practice yourself?"

"From one rink to the other," she said with a laugh.

Jackson hoisted his bag a little higher on his shoulder. "I have to get to the locker room," he said. "Are you going to be okay?"

There was a twinge of panic in my gut at being left without

Jackson. I knew my parents said Tutu was going to be fine, but what if they were wrong? What if something happened and the next phone call was… I forced the worst-case scenario out of my brain. "I'll be fine. Thank you."

"Text me if you need me, okay? Unless I'm already on the ice. Then just…hold up an SOS sign or something."

Despite the stress of the night, I laughed. "Got it. Thanks. Have a good game."

"Kick some Blackhawk ass," Lia said.

Jackson grinned and gave Lia a little salute before walking away.

I didn't even know they were playing the Blackhawks. Lia was a much better hockey girlfriend than I was.

As soon as Jackson was gone, she turned to me. "So, concession stand hot chocolate? It's the powdered stuff, but they do put marshmallows on top. My treat."

We had time to kill before the game, and it was cold in the arena. "That actually sounds amazing. Thanks."

We walked over to the concession stand, and Lia put in the order.

While we waited, I asked, "Did Jackson ask you to babysit me?"

Lia smiled. "Busted. Not babysit, but hang out with you so you wouldn't have to be alone. I was coming to the game anyway. I'm just here a little early."

"Did you have to leave your own practice?"

"I'd finished right when he texted. Perfect timing, really."

That must have been who he texted right before we got in the car to head to the rink. "Well, thank you."

A guy who looked incredibly bored handed us our Styrofoam cups of hot chocolate, and we sat down at one of the tables.

"So, it's your grandma?"

Anxiety clutched at my heart at the mention of Tutu. I

pressed the home button on my phone to make sure I hadn't missed an update from my parents. Nothing. "Yeah. She had a stroke. She had one a few years ago in Hawaii and had to come live with us, so we're pretty close."

"Is she going to be okay?" Lia asked before blowing on the steaming hot chocolate.

"I think so. But she's still in the ICU, and I assume they won't know everything for a while."

"I hope everything will be okay. But in better news, things are good between you and Jackson?"

"Yeah." I smiled. "Really good."

"I'm so glad you're finally together. Though I wasn't sure you would be when I heard about your disaster of a double date."

I winced. It wasn't exactly a memory I wanted to relive. Ever. "It was pretty bad, but the outcome was good."

"Obviously. And hey, I heard Troy and Jackson's date—Krista?—are going out. *Without* the two of you."

That information chipped away at the embarrassment that lingered from that night. Troy and Krista could be good together.

"Oh, incoming," she said, nodding toward the front doors, where the team that must have been the Blackhawks was walking inside. "See the really tall guy?"

It was easy to pick him out because he was at least a head taller than any of the other players. "Yeah."

"Number forty-two. Their best player. He's had almost as much attention from the NHL scouts as Pierce."

I made a mental note to watch for him during the game. Once the team was gone, I turned back to her. "How do you know all of that? The teams and the players and who everyone is."

She shrugged and took a sip from her cup. "You catch on pretty quickly. It's Pierce's world, you know? I want to be a part of it. So I hang around as much as possible and do some online research in my downtime. It's fun. Plus, my dad was a hockey player, so it's kind of in my blood."

"You make it look easy," I said.

"Don't worry. You'll catch on. So," she said, "how's Jackson doing on his college applications? Please tell me he's being as stubborn about it as Pierce. I can't be the only one who has to put up with this."

The question made me do the auditory version of a double take. Pierce was applying to colleges? When Jackson and I talked about college applications, it was always about me, not him. "But Jackson's hoping to be drafted. He's not interested in playing for a university. He wants to play for the NHL."

"Well, of course he does, and obviously we hope that's what happens, but what if he doesn't?"

I'd never really thought about it before. "Why is Pierce applying to universities? He's NTDP's best player. He's definitely going to be drafted, isn't he?"

Lia took a sip of her hot chocolate. "Did you see any of the games earlier this season? Not pretty. Nothing is guaranteed. Plus there's always the possibility he'll get hurt and won't be able to play anymore. Not a possibility any of us want to think about, but still. I convinced him to send in a few applications. Talk to a few coaches. He'll commit somewhere, and then obviously if he gets drafted, things will change."

"How many NTDP players usually get drafted?"

Lia shrugged. "Depends on the year. Some years, it's been a lot. Some years, especially years with bad seasons, hardly anyone. I take it from your questions that Jackson isn't very far along in the application process?"

"Actually, I'm not sure he's anywhere in that process," I said. "He's never talked to me about needing a backup plan before."

"Of course not," Lia said. "Jackson's confident and optimistic. The last thing he wants to think about is not having his dreams come true. But if he doesn't get drafted and he's not committed to a college team, the chances of him being able to enter the NHL as a free agent…"

I nodded. Not very good. Hopefully Jackson's mom was already on this, because it wasn't a conversation that I saw going very well.

At that moment, the door that led to the locker room of the main rink opened, and Jackson came running out. I hoped the fluttery feeling I got in my chest every time I saw him would never go away. He'd changed out of his shirt and tie and into his game jersey and equipment, but was still in socks, carrying his skates in his hands.

"Aren't you supposed to be warming up?" Lia asked.

He slid over to us and held up his skates. "Blades are dull. Gotta hit the pro shop to have them sharpened real quick."

"Mmhmm," Lia said, folding her arms over her chest. "Or you wanted to come check on Malina."

"Nah," he said. "But since I'm here…" He looked over at me.

"I'm fine." I held up my cup. "We're drinking hot chocolate and talking about you and Pierce."

"All good things, I hope."

"I'm telling her all of your secrets," Lia said.

But Jackson only grinned. "She's my best friend. She already knows all my secrets."

"I guess I'll have to make some up, then. Now go sharpen those skates before Coach figures out what you're really up to. I'm taking good care of Malina."

"She is," I promised.

He bent down and gave me a quick kiss. "Good. Just making sure." Then he ran off to the pro shop, skate laces trailing behind him.

Lia poked her thumbnail into the rim of her cup, making a design. "I've seen that boy with a lot of girls, but I've never seen him like that before."

Despite the stress of the day and the cold in the arena, that comment warmed me from the inside out like no hot chocolate ever could.

Unfortunately, our hot chocolate was the best thing that happened in the rink that night. NTDP lost. Three to two. Jackson let in two terrible shots before being pulled for the rest of the game. When he and Pierce walked out of the locker room after the game, hockey bags slung over their shoulders, neither of them looked thrilled.

But Jackson immediately asked, "How's Tutu?"

"She's resting," I said, which was the most recent update I'd gotten from my mom. "Sorry about the loss."

"If I could have just made one more shot," Pierce said, as if the two he did make didn't mean anything.

"That one was all my fault," Jackson said. "The shots I missed were terrible."

"Hey," Lia said, "the other team was good. You guys had an off night. Better luck next time, right?"

Pierce put an arm around his girlfriend. "I nominate you to give post-game locker room talks from now on. You didn't drop the f-bomb even once, unlike our coach."

Lia laughed. "Nomination accepted. Are you headed to dinner with the team?"

"Yeah," Pierce said. He nodded at Jackson. "You in, man?"

My heart sank. The thought of having to leave Jackson, to go home to an empty house, was one I'd been trying to avoid.

Jackson immediately looked to me. "Nah, I think I'll skip

this one. I'm going to stay with Malina."

My heart lifted, but I squashed it back down. I couldn't pull him away from a team event. I'd distracted him enough lately. "No, it's okay. I'll be fine. I'll catch up with you tomorrow."

"It's not mandatory," Jackson said. "I'll catch the next one."

"You sure?" Pierce asked.

"Positive. Don't have too much fun without me."

"Never."

Pierce and Jackson exchanged a fist bump. Lia squeezed my shoulder. "Let me know about your grandma, okay?"

"Sure. Thank you for hanging out with me. I appreciate it."

"Anytime."

We all said good-bye and headed out to the parking lot, where it was not only cold but windy. I stuffed my hands farther into my pockets for warmth.

"You okay after that loss?" I asked Jackson once we were alone.

He sighed. "Yeah. I will be. Are you doing okay?"

"Yeah." Despite the loss, the hockey game had been a good distraction for me. While he drove me home, I further distracted myself from worrying about Tutu by asking questions about NTDP players and hockey.

"The other guys have it easier," Jackson said in response to an NHL question as we turned into my neighborhood. "There can be eighteen skaters dressed for an NHL game, but only two goalies. If I would have known those odds, I might have kept playing left wing, you know?"

I didn't respond because a text came through from my mom. My lungs tightened, and I braced myself for bad news.

"Malina?" Jackson asked. "Everything okay?"

Instead of answering, I opened the text. It was a picture, so I clicked it and turned my phone to make it as large as possible. It was Tutu in a hospital bed, surrounded by all kinds of tubes and wires and machines, but smiling and making the "I love you" sign with her right hand. Gratitude made me collapse back against my seat. I choked out something that was half cry, half laugh. Like with the first stroke, her smile looked a little unnatural, but she was okay. She was going to be okay.

"What's wrong?" he demanded.

"Nothing, sorry," I said. We slowed for a stop sign, and I held the phone up for him to see.

He smiled. "She's awake? That's a good thing, right?"

"I think so," I said, and thumbed out a quick response to my mom before we pulled into my driveway.

"That Tutu is one tough cookie," Jackson said as we got out of the car and headed up to the front door. "Probably wouldn't have been a terrible hockey player back in the day."

Though I couldn't picture Tutu on skates, he was probably right. I unlocked the front door and let us inside. As I took off my shoes and coat, the quiet and emptiness in the house were almost palpable. Sure, I'd had Jackson over without my family around in the past, but that was before. It felt different now.

"Do you want something to eat?" I asked.

"No, thanks," Jackson said, heading over to the couch.

For a second, I just stood there, mouth agape. "I think that's the first time you've ever turned down food."

He laughed. "I guess there really is a first time for everything."

He patted the couch next to him, and I sat close. He reached up and tucked my hair behind my ear, toying with the strands.

"I'm glad Tutu's okay. I'm glad you were at my game. But most of all, I'm glad me and you are you and me."

I nodded to all three, my pulse picking up speed every time his hand brushed against my neck. "Me, too."

He leaned in and kissed me, skipping soft and sweet and going straight for deep and *hot*. The sharp and cool taste of mint on his tongue made me shiver. When he kissed his way down my neck to my collarbone, my heart threatened to beat right out of my rib cage. When he touched me—his hands on my neck and then sliding down my back and then slipping under the bottom of my shirt—his touch was confident yet careful and left goose bumps in its wake.

Feeling a little bit brave, I pushed him onto his back and climbed on top of him. He moaned his approval and pulled me close again, our chests rising and falling quickly against each other. Though we'd known each other for years, there was still so much to explore, and each new discovery was intoxicating—the patch of freckles on his left shoulder that I hadn't noticed before, the strong muscles in his chest and abs, the sensitive spot on his neck that made him gasp when I kissed him there. I drank it all in.

Soon we were both shirtless, and he was on top of *me*, kissing his way down my neck to my chest and back up again. I knew the science behind kissing—that oxytocin and dopamine were the reason for the flooding warmth and attraction and intense happiness I felt right then—but it didn't feel like science. It felt like magic. I let myself enjoy every touch until I tried to shift and put the attention back on him, and he suddenly backed off.

"Sorry, sorry," he said, gasping for air. "Need to take a break."

As much as I wanted to protest, it was pretty clear why he needed a break. It was nice knowing he didn't want to take things too far too soon, either.

"Okay," I said. I slipped my shirt back on and curled up next to him, which wasn't quite as nice as the kissing, but was a close second. His heart was still pounding against his rib cage.

"Can you think about hockey?" I asked.

"What?"

"You know, most guys think about baseball, but you know a lot more about hockey. Does thinking about that help...you know...distract you?"

He gave a breathy laugh. "Can't say I've ever tried it. Math is usually what works for me."

"Math?"

I felt his nod more than I saw it.

"I start doubling numbers. You know, two doubled is four, four doubled is eight, eight doubled is sixteen. By the time I get above sixteen thousand, I'm good."

I frowned and looked up at him. "You can double that high in your head?"

"It's not that hard. It doesn't take that many doubles."

"Yeah, but I'm not sure I could do that. You're smarter than you let on, aren't you?"

"I'm good at thinking things through. I did well in math when it was calculations. That changed when we had to start studying equations and rules and stuff. I couldn't be bothered after that."

"So you *are* smarter than you let on."

"Shh," he said, placing one finger lightly over my lips. "Don't tell anyone."

I laughed and put my head back on his chest. His breathing and pulse were slowing back to normal. "Don't worry. Your secret's safe with me. But speaking of being smart... Lia mentioned she's having a hard time getting Pierce to apply for college. Which made me realize something."

"That Pierce Miller is going to be drafted straight to the NHL and get to play next year without having to step foot in a college classroom?"

I rolled my eyes. Clearly the two were in cahoots. "No. I realized I haven't talked to you about applying for colleges."

"Man, you really know how to kill the mood."

"Jackson, seriously. Have you applied *anywhere*? Because I feel like that's something you would have asked for my help with or at least talked to me about."

He shrugged. "I've talked to a couple of coaches who might want me to play for them."

The fact that he hadn't even *mentioned* that to me stung—a reminder of exactly how much we'd grown apart this year. "And?" I prodded when it became clear he wasn't going to offer more information. "What did you think? Have you applied to any them? Gone on any campus tours?"

He scoffed. "I don't have time for that. It's the middle of the season. Have you seen our practice, game, and off-ice schedule? There's barely time left for school and sleep. And what little time is left, I want to spend with you."

He leaned over to kiss my neck again. My heart wanted to let him, but my brain knew this conversation needed to happen. I pulled away.

"Jackson," I said. "You can't flirt your way out of this one. If you wait until the season's over, it's going to be too late. You're going to have to think about this. Work on it."

"You sound like my mom," he grumbled.

"No, I sound like your reasonable, mature friend who wants you to succeed. Very different."

"If you say so." He squeezed my hand and then yawned. "It's late."

"Yeah," I said, feeling a twinge of disappointment that the kissing portion of the evening was probably over. "I have my interview in the morning."

"Okay," he said, but didn't make a move to get up off the couch.

"Are you going to go home?" I asked.

He smiled a little. "Actually, I might have told my mom I was staying at Pierce's house after the game. Which I can go do if you want. But if you want me to stay here so you don't have to be all alone…"

My heart lifted. That was *exactly* what I wanted. "Just sleep?"

"Just sleep," he promised. "But I'll be here if you need anything."

I leaned over and kissed him in response.

Chapter Twenty

JACKSON

Was it easy to stop myself from going too far with Malina? Hell no. But I did, because I wanted things with her to be different. So that's how I found myself in Malina's twin bed that wasn't really big enough for one of us, let alone both of us, doing nothing more than holding her and stroking my fingers up and down her arm. We both smelled like the cinnamon toothpaste in her bathroom drawer. There were glow-in-the-dark stars on the ceiling, but not just stars. Constellations. Correct constellations. I remembered she had to buy three packs to make sure she had enough of the right size stars. I loved her for that detail.

"Are you comfortable?" I asked. I was wrapped around her in a way that probably meant my arm was going to fall asleep, but I'd worry about that later.

Her head was resting against my bare chest, and she nodded. "Very."

"Good."

She shifted a little and nuzzled against me. "Jackson?"

"Yeah?"

"When do you have to leave again?"

I sighed. I didn't want to have this conversation. Yes, Malina knew I traveled a lot, but having a friend who traveled was different from having a boyfriend who traveled. Yes, I'd had girlfriends while traveling before. Lots of them. But none of them had worked out. I wanted this thing with Malina to work. I *needed* it to work in a way I hadn't needed any other relationship to work. She felt like a part of me, and losing her would be like losing a limb. And not a toe or a finger or something. Like a whole leg.

"Next week," I said. "Travel is kind of crazy coming up. I think I'm in Vancouver, Milwaukee, Des Moines, Pittsburg, and Montreal. Lots of away games. This week is really the last 'vacation' I get all season."

"Oh." She didn't say anything else for a minute. "What about Thanksgiving? You'll be home then, right?"

The hope in her voice crushed me with guilt. "We're scheduled to get home late Wednesday night, then I'm spending half the day with my mom and half the day with my dad, then we leave again Friday morning." As much as I didn't want that to sound like "I don't have time to spend with you," that was exactly what it ended up sounding like. Most of the time, I was the guy who broke up with girls right before holidays so I wouldn't have to worry about plans and gifts and all of that. This was the first holiday season that I actually *wanted* to spend time with someone, but my schedule wouldn't allow it. "Sorry, but—"

"It's fine," she said around a yawn. "We'll see each other when you get home. And you'll have some home games in December, right? And some time off over Christmas and New Year's?"

"Yeah," I said, but I was lying. There were a couple of

home games, and I did get a little time off, but not very much. When I thought about after the holidays, my schedule got even worse. It was the heart of hockey season, plus playoffs, plus our international tournament. The pressure would also be on the closer we got to the NHL draft, too. Not to mention, what would happen at the end of the season? At the end of the year? Malina would be off to...somewhere, and where would I be?

Normally, this would be when I'd say it wasn't worth it, that we should break up and save ourselves the trouble, but that was the last thing I wanted to do. Instead, I found myself wanting to find, or make, some kind of reality in which Malina and I could be together despite all of those challenges.

If only it were that easy.

"Jackson?" Malina asked.

The way she said my name made it pretty clear it wasn't the first time she'd said it. "Sorry, what?"

"Thank you. For this. For tonight."

I pushed all of that stuff about the future aside and kissed the top of her head. "You're welcome."

We were quiet for a minute or two. Then I said, "Malina?"

No response.

When I looked down, her eyes were closed and her chest was rising and falling slowly and evenly. Not quite ready to fall asleep yet, I grabbed my phone. I'd missed a few texts while my phone was on silent, so I thumbed into my messages.

Pierce: *Holy shit. Guess who is at the same restaurant as us?*

Pierce: *Ben. Demarco. He was at the game.*

Heat rushed through my veins. Ben Demarco was a scout from the Philadelphia Flyers. It was no secret that they'd be looking for a new backup goalie for next season.

Pierce: *He just asked about you. Dude, where are you?? Get down here!*

My grip tightened around my phone. Ben Demarco had seen one of my worst games of the season, yet still asked about me afterward, and I wasn't there to meet him?

Pierce: *He left. Cool guy. Wish you had been here. Hope Malina is okay.*

The timestamp on the texts made my stomach sink. There wasn't any point in responding anymore. Even though scouts couldn't do anything official yet, everyone knew it was the unofficial meetings, the personal connections, that really counted, and I'd missed an opportunity with the team I'd been hoping for most of all. My sister had even gotten me a Flyers jersey for my birthday. Now every time I opened my closet and saw the familiar black and orange logo, I'd feel like an idiot.

I scrubbed a hand across my face. It wasn't only the missed opportunity, though. I'd played terribly today. I'd been distracted—trying to get a glimpse of Malina in the stands had cost me at least one of those goals—and no doubt Demarco had seen it, too. Slacking on my workouts hadn't helped, either. And why had I been slacking on my workouts?

Malina.

I'd thought I could make things work with her—I desperately *wanted* to make things work with her—but instead, everything was falling apart. I knew being with her wouldn't be like being with the other girls I dated, but I'd been thinking with my heart, not my brain. I had to do something to stop the bleeding before things got worse.

Before I lost everything I'd worked for.

Malina curled into me in her sleep. Shit. How could I do this to her? Especially now?

No. There had to be another way. I could turn things around, couldn't I? We could talk about it in the morning. Or maybe after Tutu was better. Malina would know what to do. She had to be as distracted as I was, and she had just as much on the line. Maybe she'd be okay with a break so we could get our shit together.

I set my phone aside, kissed the top of Malina's head, and followed her into sleep.

Chapter Twenty-One

MALINA

Something tugged at my brain, pulling me out from under layers of sleep. It was a literal fight to consciousness as my body battled with my mind. When I opened my eyes, I realized why the battle was so tough: I was possibly the most comfortable I'd ever been, curled up against Jackson, safe in his arms. When I looked up, he was sound asleep, only possibly not quite as comfortable. His head had slipped off my pillow, and was tipped at an angle that was definitely going to leave him with a stiff neck when he woke up.

Jackson's phone buzzed insistently on my dresser. That must have been what woke me up. The way it was buzzing, someone must have been calling him, not messaging. When it stopped vibrating and started right up again almost immediately, I sat up a little to see who was calling.

Jackson stirred in his sleep, but didn't wake. Pierce's name and picture were on the screen. But my gaze quickly drifted from Pierce's name to the time shown at the top of the screen.

No. That couldn't be right. I blinked hard and willed my vision to clear.

Pierce's call ended, and the screen went black. I frantically jabbed at the home button, looking for the correct time on the lock screen, but it was still the same.

10:46. Until the minute changed to 10:47.

No. No, no, no.

Jackson's phone must have still been set to some weird time zone from his travels. It couldn't have possibly been 10:47. We couldn't possibly have slept that long. I frantically searched for my phone. Surely that would've been right. Surely it would've shown that I had time to shower and look my best and get to my interview with plenty of time to spare.

As I dug through the sheets, where I must have dropped the phone before we fell asleep, Jackson woke up. Before his eyes were even open, he winced and reached for his neck.

"Jackson, move," I said, pushing him to the side so I could check under him.

"Ow," he said, voice thick with sleep. "What? What's wrong?"

"What time is it? I can't find my phone, and the time on your phone is wrong."

"What? What are you talking about?"

When he leaned forward to grab his phone, my fingers made contact with the case of my phone. I pulled it out from between the sheets. Jabbed at the home button. And my heart stopped.

It was 10:47. My alarm had gone off. It was there in the notifications. But the phone had been buried too deep to wake me from sleep. Dread started at the tip of my skull and worked its way through my veins all the way down to my toes.

"I missed the interview," I said. "We overslept, and I missed the interview." The words came out so much calmer than I felt.

"And I missed practice," Jackson said, still rubbing at his neck. "*Shit.*"

"I have to go. Maybe they'll still take me late…maybe they'll understand…maybe they'll…" I jumped out of bed and threw on the closest outfit I could find—a pair of jeans and a rumpled shirt. My hands shook as I buttoned the jeans. I was supposed to wear a dress. Not this. But it was too late to change that. I had to leave. I ran down to the kitchen to grab the keys to my mom's car, but they weren't on the counter where Dad usually left them. The sick feeling in my stomach doubled.

"Seven missed calls. Twenty missed texts. Coach is *pissed*," Jackson said as he thundered down the stairs.

I ignored him and ran to see if the keys were on the hook by the door. They weren't.

Meanwhile, Jackson was pacing back and forth, phone still in his hand. "I knew this would happen."

I went to the desk and started opening one drawer after another. His overreaction coupled with the distinct lack of keys in each drawer caused my chest to tighten with each too-shallow breath. I slammed a drawer shut. "You knew we'd oversleep? Well, you could have helped me out by setting an alarm!"

"No. I knew being with you would get in the way of hockey. I knew I couldn't do both."

Rage boiled under my skin. It wasn't just that I couldn't believe Jackson had said something that awful on one of the worst mornings of my life. It was that I couldn't believe he'd said it at all. "Seriously? I'm messing with your *hockey* career? You missed one practice! So what? Go late and apologize. It's *one practice*! You have like a thousand of them. I missed a one-shot, potentially life-changing interview! Do you realize that? Do you even care?" I slammed the final drawer shut. "What the hell did my parents do with the damn keys?"

Jackson's gaze snapped up from his phone. "Coach doesn't play games. If you're even five minutes late, you're not allowed in the rink. And I'll probably be benched for the next game. There are going to be scouts there, and I won't be able to play."

I abandoned my search for the keys. "Yeah, well, maybe this is why you needed a freaking backup plan. So that if being with me caused you such a problem that you got benched and didn't make an NHL team, you could still go to college. But no. You're too good for backup plans. Well, guess what? That's not how it works. Life isn't one big party where you get everything you want."

"Hey, at least I'm going for my dreams. Your entire *life* is a backup plan. You're not even trying for what you really want."

The words were a slap in the face that knocked all of the air out of my lungs. Maybe Jackson had hinted at the idea before, but he'd never put it so bluntly.

He threw his hands up in frustration. "I mean, you're freaking out right now about a scholarship interview for a program and career that you don't even *want*! What is that about?"

"It's called being realistic," I snapped. "It's called thinking about the future, something you clearly don't get. I really thought our relationship could be different. That we could last longer than two weeks, unlike your first thousand relationships, but I guess I was wrong." I folded my arms over my chest. If he could go for the low blow, then so could I.

"I guess you were. You know, I'd offer you a ride," he said, "but I don't want any part in helping you settle."

"Fine," I spat. "I don't want a ride from you anyway."

"Good. Besides, I have to go try to apologize to Coach. To tell him my girlfriend was the reason I was late, but the girlfriend thing won't be a problem anymore."

"No. It won't. Until you're on to the next girl. Which will be when, tomorrow?"

He gave an angry shrug. "It's still early. Why not tonight?"

Glaring at him, I said what I should have said all along. "Get out of my house."

"Fine. Good-bye, Malina."

Without another word or even a backward glance, he was gone. That meant I could focus on what I needed to focus on: getting to the interview. Of course, when I focused on that, I remembered the text my mom sent saying she'd forgotten the keys in her jacket pocket. I found them, grabbed my paperwork for the interview along with my purse, and dashed out of the house.

After quickly putting the address into the maps system, I started driving as fast as possible while also checking for cops. The last thing this day needed was a speeding ticket. When I arrived, I took the first parking space I saw, got out of the car, and started running.

This wasn't how it was supposed to be. I was supposed to be dressed nicely, walking calmly, my only concern being what I was going to say in the interview. And from what my dad said, that wouldn't have been much of a concern at all. Instead, I was tearing up at the thought that I'd thrown it all away.

I threw the door open and ran up to the desk with the scholarship sign.

"Can I help you?" the woman asked. She was dressed in a neat suit, hair and makeup perfect. The only thing off about her was her concerned expression as she studied my disheveled appearance.

The look brought even more tears to my eyes. I ran my hands over my shirt again. "Yes, I'm Malina Hall. I had an interview scheduled for ten o'clock, and I'm so sorry I'm late, but I was wondering if there was any way I could still do the interview."

The woman gave me a sad smile. "I'm sorry, but we have back-to-back interviews scheduled all day." She nodded toward a row of chairs, where a few much more put-together than me high schoolers were waiting. "There are many students who are here on time. Was there some kind of emergency?"

For two seconds, I thought about explaining what had happened to Tutu, but that wasn't the real reason I was late. I couldn't stoop to that level. "No, there wasn't. I'm really, really sorry, but please. Can I interview at the end of the day? I'll stay here all day. I'll do anything."

The woman's smile disappeared. "I'm sorry, Ms. Hall, but if you can't arrive at an interview on time, how do we know that you'll be fully dedicated to your studies or to a career with us someday? It's one of our rules."

I wanted to break out the "my dad works for your company" line, but I couldn't stoop to that level, either. "Okay," I said, but didn't move. My limbs were frozen as my brain struggled to catch up to reality.

"If there's nothing else, there's someone behind you waiting to check in."

I turned. I hadn't even heard someone else come up. The guy was wearing a suit. He was probably an hour early for his interview. Yeah, he deserved it more than I did. "Good luck," I said to him. He thanked me as I walked away.

I was so numb that I barely felt my legs moving. When I got in the car and closed the door, the silence washed over me. What was I going to tell my dad? What was I going to do without the one scholarship I'd really been banking on? How had I lost Jackson, not just as a boyfriend, but as a friend?

I let my head fall against the steering wheel and cried.

Chapter Twenty-Two

As predicted, Coach had not let me step one blade on the ice, and also promised to bench me for the next game. It had been a while since someone had been late to a practice, so the guys gave me a hard time as I left. They were joking around — I wasn't the first person to be late, and I probably wouldn't be the last — but I wasn't in a joking mood. I ignored their comments and left the rink, slamming the door on my way out.

While I drove home, I couldn't stop thinking about the argument with Malina. I stomped on the gas pedal. I was going too fast, but couldn't bring myself to care. What was she thinking when she said all of that shit? She knew exactly who I was when she let us be more than friends. How could she throw that back in my face? And when it came to my future, how could she not believe in me? Wasn't that what girlfriends were supposed to do? What *friends* were supposed to do? Believe in you and support you no matter what? My stomach burned with the fact that she obviously didn't.

And yeah, maybe I hadn't said things to her very nicely, but they needed to be said. In fact, I probably should have said them a long time ago.

When I got home, I opened the front door and slammed it hard enough that the painting on the wall rattled. My muscles and brain craved more of that release. A workout was definitely needed to get out some of this frustration. And since I wouldn't be getting out any energy during practice or during the next game…

"Lukey? Is that you?"

It sounded like Mom, but she didn't call me that. I trudged into the living room, where my sister was sitting on the couch, piles of folded and unfolded laundry all around her.

"Hey!" She set the laundry aside and jumped up to give me a hug, throwing her arms around my neck. "God, would you quit getting taller?"

I forced my anger down a notch. Lacey didn't deserve for me to take any of this out on her. "I'll work on that. What are you doing home?"

She sat back down and started folding a shirt. "My roommate's boyfriend came into town this morning, so I wanted to give them some space."

"Ah. Very considerate you."

"I like to think so. Hey, I thought Mom said you had practice this morning?"

I took a seat on the couch next to her. The second I did, some of my anger shifted to self-pity that pooled in the pit of my stomach. On second thought, maybe I wouldn't work out. Maybe I'd take advantage of the day off to do nothing but binge watch a show on Netflix and eat my body weight in Doritos and donuts. "Yes, but I was late so Coach kicked me out."

Lacey frowned and messed with the sloppy bun on top

of her head. "Late to practice? You? How did that happen?"

"I overslept."

"Didn't you spend the night at Pierce's house? Was he late, too?"

I winced. "Well, no. Because I wasn't actually at Pierce's house. That's just what I told Mom."

"And in reality, you were…"

"At Malina's house." Even saying her name stung.

"Ah," she said. "Sounds like karma got you on that lie."

I sighed. "Yeah. I wasn't allowed to practice and have to sit the bench the next game."

"Tough break, kiddo. I bet you won't let that happen again."

"No," I said. What I *didn't* say was that it *couldn't* happen again, because I'd lost Malina entirely, not only as my girlfriend, but also as my friend. I toyed with the sleeve of one of the yet-to-be-folded shirts.

After a minute or two of silence, Lacey asked, "Is that all?"

I glanced down at her. "What do you mean?"

"Well, I know you're disappointed about practice and the game, but you seem more than disappointed. You seem sad."

With a sigh, I let the sleeve drop from between my fingers. Talking about this sounded worse than doing wind sprints. There wasn't any point in talking. It wouldn't make me feel better. But knowing Lacey and her convincing lawyer-ish ways, I figured I should probably get it over with. "Malina and I had a fight. I think we're done."

She frowned. "You two fought?"

"Yeah."

"After you spent the night at her house?"

"Yeah."

"About what?"

The anger that had settled rose right back up to the

surface. "She said all this crap about me, about how I can't stay in a relationship and how I'm not serious about anything and treat life like one big party."

Her frown deepened. "Malina said all of that? Malina Hall? That doesn't sound like her."

I shrugged one shoulder against the back of the couch. Maybe that was what stung most of all: that Malina wasn't who I thought she was all those years of our friendship. It was like I'd lost all of those years, too. "Apparently it is."

Lacey sat back, crossed one leg over the other, and folded her hands like she was pre-psychiatry instead of pre-law. "Okay, okay. Back up. I'm going to need some context here. So you were at her house, I'm assuming everything was fine before you fell asleep because you stayed the night, but you woke up, and then…?"

My stomach clenched. I didn't want to go through this again. What was done was done. What was said was said. "I don't know."

"Luke," Lacey said in her "calling me on my bullshit" tone. Mom had that exact same tone.

I threw my hands up in defeat. "Fine. We woke up late, and I was freaking out because I missed practice, and she was freaking out because she missed some scholarship interview."

"What kind of scholarship interview?"

"One for her dad's company, I think."

Lacey gasped. "She had an interview for that huge scholarship? It's a big deal to even get that opportunity."

"I guess," I said, but it wasn't a big deal because Malina didn't even want to go into business. Maybe it was a big deal for people who did, but not for her.

"Oh no. Poor Malina. Would they take her late?"

My defenses flew up hard and fast. "I don't know. But this is about me, not Malina."

"Right," Lacey said. "Sorry. She missed her interview.

You missed practice. Continue."

"Okay, so I was trying to calm her down, you know? Reminding her it's one scholarship and she's applying for like a million of them. She's going to be fine. So then she freaks out on me and how I'm not applying for anything and how I can't be serious about anything and she shouldn't be surprised that our relationship isn't going to last."

Lacey winced. "Ouch."

I stood and started pacing back and forth in front of the couch, frustration preventing me from sitting still any longer. "Yeah. I mean, it's one thing for some girl I'm dating to say all of that. It's another thing for my best friend to say it."

"It still doesn't sound like her. What did you say to her?"

The question made me trip over thin air, stumbling a step before I caught myself. "Nothing! This isn't my fault! It's not my fault we overslept and she missed her interview and was pissed about that."

"I know, I know," Lacey said. "And yeah, her disappointment probably did influence the things she said. But you were probably upset about missing practice, which means you might have said things you normally wouldn't have, too. Maybe she was a little offended when you said it was one scholarship? It might not seem that way to you, but to her it was probably a pretty big deal."

Guilt formed a lump in my throat. No matter what I thought, it probably *was* a big deal to her, and it *definitely* was a big deal to her dad, who was sitting at the hospital with Tutu, who had just had a stroke. Shit. I hadn't thought about any of that before opening my mouth, and that wasn't the only negative thing I'd said. I ran a hand through my hair and let out a tense sigh.

"What are you thinking, little brother?" Lacey asked.

I swallowed around the lump in my throat. "I said some other things that I maybe shouldn't have, at least not right then."

She made a "go ahead" motion with her hand.

"I told her that she was getting in the way of my hockey career. Then I called her out on not going into what she really wants to go into. For going with the safe plan and going into business when really she wants to go into astrophysics. And yeah, maybe I was mad and that wasn't the time or way to say it, but that one needed to be said. She's playing it safe, and she has no reason for that. She's too smart for that."

"Like you're too smart to not even consider trying to go to college?"

The words were a knife to my chest. "Wait, why are you taking her side? I'm your *brother*."

She shook her head. "Not taking her side. Just showing you that there are two ways to look at every situation. And she does have a point that things are changing. You had a blast in high school, and it's easy to think and hope nothing is going to change, but I'll be the first to tell you the real world is different. Some things are bigger and more important than fun. Like attending a good college. Like Malina. I mean, you two were best friends for years. Are you sure you want to let this one argument ruin that for you?"

On the surface, I did. I wanted to fold my arms over my chest and pout and stay mad at her forever. Below the surface, where Lacey was poking holes in my logic left and right, I knew I couldn't do that. The problem was that even though my mind was whirling a thousand miles an hour, it wasn't landing on a solution. "So what am I supposed to do?"

Lacey smiled. "You're smart. You'll figure it out. And in the meantime"—she set a stack of shirts in my lap—"you can fold these."

Chapter Twenty-Three

MALINA

When I got home from the non-interview, I sat down on the couch, shoes still on, useless paperwork still in my hands. Everything felt numb, from my fingers to my heart to my brain. As soon as I thought about having to tell my dad what happened, my eyes burned and the tears started again. Tears for missing the interview. Tears for losing Jackson. Tears because I felt both guilty and sorry for myself, and there wasn't really a worse combination of emotions.

When my phone dinged in my purse, I jumped, startled out of my emotional mess. I wiped my eyes, took out my phone, and opened the messages from my mom. The good news was that Tutu had been moved out of ICU and to a regular room, where she would spend a couple of days.

Me: *Can I come visit?*

Mom: *Of course. Drive safely. Text me when you get here, and I'll bring you up.*

So I buried my useless paperwork deep in the garbage can, where I wouldn't have to be reminded about what happened today, and tried my best to bury the sick feeling in my stomach, too.

The drive was actually good for me. I put on some music, followed the GPS directions, and tried not to think about much else. It wasn't until I arrived at the hospital and found visitor parking that I felt butterflies in my stomach. But not good butterflies. Poisonous ones. My mom had updated me on Tutu's condition, but seeing her in person was a whole different story. And what was I going to tell my parents about the interview?

When I walked up to the hospital entrance, my mom was already standing there.

"Hey," I said, giving her a big hug, soaking in some of the comfort I knew we both needed. "How is she?"

Mom looked tired, but she was smiling. "Excited to see you. Come on."

She motioned me through the sliding doors toward the elevator. While we walked and waited, I asked questions about Tutu's condition to delay the inevitable question about my interview. No reason to have to tell that story more than once. And I knew the question would be the first words out of my dad's mouth.

"She's mostly having trouble with her left arm and leg," Mom said as we stepped off the elevator. The hallway smelled strongly like soap and some kind of lemon cleaner. "But her speech hasn't been affected much this time. You'll see."

The butterflies in my stomach grew more restless as we walked down the hall, but they settled down the second we walked into the room and Tutu smiled at me.

"Lina," she said.

Those butterflies flew away completely. Mom was right. She was okay. That was what mattered most of all.

"Hey, Tutu," I said, walking over to her bed and giving her a gentle hug, careful to avoid the tubes and wires around her. When I leaned back, I said, "You scared me."

"*Maika'i au*," Tutu said. She was fine. "Don't worry."

"Doesn't she look great?" Dad asked.

I slipped the bracelet Tutu had weaved off my wrist and onto hers. Just to give her something other than the gray hospital gown and white sheets. "She looks beautiful," I said, and Tutu beamed.

"So, how was the interview?" Dad asked.

Every muscle in my body tightened. Okay, so it was the *second* question out of his mouth. I took a shaky breath. "I missed the interview."

"You *what*?" Dad demanded. "What happened? Did you get in an accident? Was there some kind of emergency?"

The tears that had passed while I drove there filled my eyes again. "I overslept. Slept through my alarm. I went late, but they wouldn't take me. I'm really sorry."

"You *overslept*?" Dad asked. "This was your ticket not only to college but to a future career, and you *slept through your alarm*? How in the world did you happen?"

My cheeks burned as badly as my eyes. I knew this was going to be bad, but there was no way to be prepared for this kind of anger and disappointment.

"Hey, guys, let's talk about this in the hall," Mom said, clearly not wanting to upset Tutu. "*Makuahine*, we'll be right back."

Tutu waved us off, and we walked into the hall. It took all of my energy to look at my dad instead of the floor. He was so clearly upset. So hurt. And I hadn't even told him the whole story.

"There's something else," I said.

"What?" Dad asked. "What else could you possibly have to say right now?"

"The reason I overslept was because Jackson was over. He spent the night so I wouldn't have to be alone. Nothing happened, but we must have fallen asleep before I could make sure my alarm was on and loud enough."

"Jackson?" my dad hissed.

If there had been any muscles in my body that weren't tight before, they were then. Maybe it was good I had told them in a public location. He couldn't really yell. Couldn't try to murder me. Or if he had, I was already in a hospital.

"I'm so, so sorry," I said. "I know that doesn't help, and I know there's nothing I can do to fix this, but I am really sorry."

"I can't believe this. I can't believe you threw away—"

"Hey, how about you and I talk in the waiting room?" Mom suggested, gently but still loudly enough to interrupt my father's tirade. "Malina, why don't you go sit with Tutu? Let us know if she needs anything."

My body relaxed the tiniest bit. Mom was going to try to talk dad off the ledge for me. I wiped at my eyes again and nodded before walking back into Tutu's room. Her eyes were closed, but she opened them the second I sat in the visitor's chair. She used her right hand to motion me closer. When I did, she reached out and patted my arm.

"Sorry," I said. "Didn't mean to cause drama."

Tutu shrugged. "The hospital is boring."

"Not anymore," I said, wondering what my mom was saying to my dad.

"It will be okay, Malina. You are a smart woman. You'll still go to a good school. You'll still get a good job."

What she didn't know was that it wasn't just that. It was that the plan I'd been working toward for so long felt dumb, and anything more than that felt impossible, despite what Jackson had said. "Yeah, but I don't want just a good job."

"What do you mean?" Tutu asked.

"I mean I don't want to go into business. I don't want to

get a safe job. I want to go into astrophysics."

That must have been one of those words that didn't translate well into Hawaiian, and it must not have been used much in English there, because Tutu frowned at me, the left side of her mouth dipping a tiny bit lower than the right.

"Studying space," I said. "I want to go to a technical school and study space as an astrophysicist."

"Ah, space," she said with a nod. "You always loved space. You didn't always love business."

"Exactly."

"So study space."

I had to smile at her nonchalant tone. "It's not that easy."

"Why not?"

I bit my lip. "Because not many schools have astrophysics programs. The ones that do are ridiculously hard to get into, and I missed the early application deadlines. And yeah, careers in astrophysics are amazing, but they're really competitive. I'd never be able to get one, and then I'd have an expensive degree and no job, which isn't exactly ideal." Another tear rolled down my cheek and landed on the leg of my pants. The self-pity tears seemed bigger than all the rest.

"Hey," Tutu said, and motioned for me to lean closer.

I did, and she wiped at my tears with one shaky thumb. "You are smart. Brilliant."

"No I'm not, I can't even—"

"Ah, ah, ah," she said. "I'll talk. You listen."

My cheeks flushed. I knew better than to argue with her. Plus, Tutu beat the odds not once, but twice. I needed to be grateful she was okay and soak up every bit of wisdom from her that I could.

"You are *smart*. And it's only November. It's not too late."

She was right. Even if I'd missed early applications, regular applications were still open.

"Most of all, you are hard working. You do what you set

your mind to. The problem here is you set your mind to the wrong thing. You did not go after your dreams. If you don't do that, they don't come true."

"You sound like Jackson," I mumbled. And really, if Jackson and Tutu were saying the same thing, maybe they were right. Maybe I owed it to them to consider trying. The thought made me feel kind of sick.

"Jackson's smart, too. Smarter than he thinks."

Talking about Jackson brought memories of our argument back to the surface. The ache of knowing I'd probably lost him ran all the way down to my bones. "Jackson and I got in a fight."

She frowned again. "You fought? Why?"

I went through everything with her, about how he didn't seem to care at all that I'd missed my interview and how he'd said the whole "getting in the way of hockey" and "not going after my dreams" things, but in not nearly as nice of a way. I even confessed about the not-quite-so-nice things I'd said about him and his past, present, and future.

"Sounds like both of you need to apologize," Tutu said.

"Maybe." The problem was that I didn't know if he'd even talk to me, and I certainly didn't know how to start the conversation. Or finish it, for that matter. Did I want to be done with him? Did I want to try to make this work? Would he be willing to try to make up? His track record showed that he tended to wave the white flag and call it quits as soon as things got rough. My chest ached with the knowledge that things between us had gotten so rough so quickly and might never be right again.

"Tell him no more food from me until he makes this right with you."

I laughed. That actually had a chance of working. If anything could save Luke Jackson, it was definitely food, especially Tutu's food. "I'll tell him that."

Tutu closed her eyes again.

"Are you tired?" I asked.

"Just need a little rest," she said.

"Okay. I'll be right here when you wake up." I stood and placed a kiss on the top of her head.

A few minutes later, when I thought she was already asleep, Tutu said, "Malina?"

"Yeah?" I asked, ready to go grab my parents or a nurse if she needed something.

"Missing this interview? It's not the end of the world. It is the beginning."

That made me tear up for an entirely different reason. Maybe she was right. Maybe I needed a nudge to knock me out of my comfort zone, and missing the interview was exactly that nudge. "Thanks, Tutu."

She didn't say anything else, but she didn't need to.

Chapter Twenty-Four

After hanging out with Lacey for a while, I went down to the basement to work out. I always thought better when I was on the treadmill or lifting weights. It was like getting the blood pumping also made my brain work better. I set the treadmill to a jog to warm up. My muscles warmed quickly even in the cold basement. While I picked the speed up from a jog to a run, I thought.

This was far from the first time I'd had an argument with a girl, but it was the first time I couldn't get it out of my brain. Normally this would be the time when I'd be moving on to find some other girl. But I didn't want to move on. I didn't want some other girl. I'd say it was because Malina and I were friends first, but I'd dated girls who were friends before, and I'd never felt like this. There was something else going on.

Once I'd gotten a few miles in, I slowed to a walk to get ready to lift weights. On my way over to the bench, I noticed something out of the corner of my eye. There was a piece of paper on the ground, underneath the card table I'd set up for Malina and hadn't put away yet. Still breathing hard from my run, I walked over and picked it up. It looked like a sheet of notes had fallen out of her bag in her frantic attempt to clean up when my mom interrupted us. It didn't look too important—some essay topics and notes in her neat handwriting. At the top of the page, where most people would draw doodles or squiggles or something meaningless, Malina had drawn a constellation, dashed lines connecting stars in a shape I didn't recognize but knew she knew everything about. Man, I loved this girl.

I loved this girl.

My heart started to race even though I wasn't doing anything more strenuous than standing there, holding a piece of paper. I loved Malina. That was the difference between her and all of the girls who had come before. It wasn't only that we were friends. It was that I loved her and couldn't possibly let the argument we'd had be the end.

I needed a plan. I needed a way to fix all of the things I'd messed up. I could try to apologize to her. I wasn't very good with words, especially apologies, but this one would be worth it.

But that idea still didn't sit right with me. I didn't want to *tell* her I was sorry and was in this for the long haul. There was a good chance she wouldn't believe me. I wanted to *show* her those things. As I hit the weights, an idea formed. There was one thing I could do. I didn't have any clue if it would work. It might end up being a disaster. But if it did work...it might be enough. It had to be enough. I finished my workout, showered, and started putting my plan into motion.

Malina's room was on the second floor, facing the driveway.

Her bedroom light was on, and I saw occasional flickers of movement, so I was pretty sure she was up there. There were also lights on downstairs, so I assumed at least one of her parents was home. Perfect. I parked down the street, got out of my car, walked up to the front door, and knocked quietly.

It took a minute or two, but then Mr. Hall opened the door. Several emotions quickly crossed his face: surprise, unhappiness, anger, and confusion. It was pretty obvious he knew more about what had happened than I wanted him to know.

"Good evening, Mr. Hall," I said. "How's Tutu?"

"She's doing okay. Better than you'll be doing if you think you're going to spend the night again or even look at my daughter tonight."

A rush of heat washed over me despite the cold air. He knew a *lot* more than I wanted him to know. "Mr. Hall, you have every right in the world to be mad at me. So does Malina. But I assure you that my intentions were good. I didn't want her to be alone after what happened. It was completely innocent."

"Innocent would have been calling a friend to stay with her. A *girl* friend. Good night, Jackson."

"Wait," I said.

By some miracle, he did.

"I know I messed up. I owe Malina an apology. I figured she wouldn't necessarily listen to how sorry I am, so I wanted to show her. That's why I'm here. Not to talk to her. To do something for her."

Mr. Hall's expression changed very slightly from anger to curiosity. He motioned for me to come in so he could close the door.

"Explain," he said.

I kept my voice as quiet as possible. "I know she's stressed and hasn't been able to get her STEM project to work. I want to look at it. See if there's anything I can do to help."

Mr. Hall scoffed. "Malina has worked on that for months. You think you can fix it in a few minutes?"

My face warmed. Of course the plan probably sounded idiotic. It probably *was* idiotic. But I had to try. "I'll work on it all night if I have to. I want to show her that I'm not giving up on her, and she shouldn't give up on herself. Plus, I have a trick up my sleeve."

He narrowed his eyebrows. "What kind of trick?"

"A brilliant friend who's waiting for my call. Please, Mr. Hall. Let me stay and work on this for her. Let me apologize."

He considered it for a long time. Too long. I squirmed under his stare. But finally, he nodded. "Okay. But mostly because I'm curious. And because, even though she made some terrible decisions, I still love my daughter."

Relief washed over me. The hardest part was over. Well, at least the hardest part except the reason I was there. "Thank you."

He hesitated before walking away. "You should know that I'll be sleeping with the door open. And I'm a very light sleeper."

"I'm not going to step foot upstairs. I don't even want her to know I'm here."

"Good," he said. "Get to work."

With quiet footsteps, I walked into the living room and over to the planets. It looked like everything I'd need was there...all of her materials, her laptop, even some notes. It was overwhelming, like trying to play hockey in a pitch-black rink while using a pool cue and a ping-pong ball instead of a puck and a stick.

I powered up the laptop. Thankfully, I knew her password, which she hadn't changed in years. I also knew enough to know which program she was working in. The first thing I did was back up the file, so that if I broke anything, there would be an automatic reset available. Then I powered up the project and started it, hoping that maybe I'd stumble upon some beginner's luck. That maybe all that was needed was for someone different to try the program on a different day. But like Malina had said, only the rotation of the planets, around their axes and around the sun, worked. The lights stayed off. I fumbled my way through the code, and after a few false starts, I figured out how to turn off the rotation and ran the program again. This time, the lights worked. It really was beautiful, with the sun giving off the majority of the light, and the other planets giving off varying amounts depending on their location and whatever other factors Malina had studied. My pride swelled over how much she'd accomplished so far. The lights even dimmed and brightened and shifted on a semi-regular schedule, as if they were supposed to rotate, but couldn't.

A quiet throat clearing made me jump. Thankfully, it wasn't Malina, but Mr. Hall. He held out a mug to me.

"Thought you might need some coffee."

I accepted the peace offering. "Definitely. Thank you."

He nodded and let me return to work. My eyes and head started to ache as I struggled to catch up to the places Malina had spent weeks and months getting to. I was so caught up in the work that I almost didn't hear Mr. Hall say, "What do you need to go downstairs for?"

Instantly, my heart shot into my throat. It was late enough that Malina should have been getting ready to go to bed—she was definitely an "early to bed, early to rise" kind of person—but those were her footsteps on the stairs. I jumped up and ran over to the armchair, diving behind it so that if she looked in the living room, she wouldn't be able to see me.

"I need to get my laptop. I guess I need to start looking for more scholarships."

Shit. If she went for her computer and saw that it was on

and open to the project program, my plan would fall apart. All I could do was hope and pray that Mr. Hall would be able and willing to stall somehow.

"Malina," he said, "you had a rough day. I know you're still upset, and I know you're tired. Is now really the time to be looking for more scholarships? Is that really putting your best foot forward? Why don't you call it a night and start fresh again tomorrow?"

There was a pause—too long of a pause.

"I don't know," she said. "I—"

"Why don't you go on upstairs? I'll bring you some of that tea Tutu makes to help you sleep."

"Why are you spoiling me when I messed up so badly?" she asked.

"Because I realized that everyone makes mistakes. Even me. Now head on up. I'll be right there."

A second later, I heard Malina's footsteps retreating up the stairs. The anxious pit that had formed in my stomach disappeared. I gave myself a few extra seconds, then poked my head up over the armchair. Mr. Hall was standing there with a smile on his face, like he was incredibly proud of what he'd done.

"How's that for distraction?" he asked.

"Amazing," I said. "Thank you."

Then I headed back to work while he went to the kitchen to make tea.

I continued studying for a while, getting acclimated and making sure Malina was, in fact, going to sleep. Finally, when the house was completely quiet and I'd gotten about as far as I could without any assistance, I took my phone out of my pocket. I tapped into my contacts and started a FaceTime call. It only took a second for Troy's face to appear on the screen.

"You're in?" he asked.

I adjusted the volume so I could hear him, but definitely

no one else in the house could. "I'm in, and so far outside of my comfort zone, I don't even remember what my comfort zone looks like."

"Sometimes that's what it takes to get the girl," he said.

"Yeah. And sometimes it takes the help of a friend."

Troy rubbed his hands together. "Okay. Let's do this."

Chapter Twenty-Five

MALINA

When I woke up the first time on Sunday morning, I remembered everything that had happened the day before, groaned, rolled over, and went back to sleep so I wouldn't have to deal with reality for a little while longer.

When I woke up the second time, the house smelled like coffee and pancakes. As much as I didn't want to face the day and deal with the mess I'd made, making things right would be a lot easier to do with caffeine and sugary syrup.

I sighed, stretched, and unplugged my phone from the charger on my dresser. For a second, I let myself believe that I'd have an email saying I could reschedule the interview. Or a text from Jackson saying that everything yesterday had been a mistake and we could make it through this. Or both. Instead, there was neither. Just a text from Izzy, asking how the interview went.

As much as I loved the girl, I couldn't deal with responding to that text right then. She'd have to wait. I threw off the covers, went to the bathroom, and headed downstairs.

Dad was flipping pancakes at the stove. "Good morning," he said, glancing over his shoulder. "Did you sleep well?"

Despite the stress of the day, I *had* slept well. Maybe being that stressed out was not only emotionally exhausting, but also physically exhausting. "Yeah, I did. Thanks. How's Tutu?"

"Well, she complained about the hospital breakfast, so I guess that's a good sign."

It was a good sign, and I'd take it.

"Pancakes will be ready soon," Dad said.

There wasn't any hint of the anger or frustration from the day before in his voice. Whatever my mom had said to him in that hospital waiting room must have been the right thing to say. I grabbed my favorite mug, filled it most of the way with coffee, and then added enough flavored creamer from the fridge so it wouldn't actually taste like coffee. When I closed the fridge, Dad was waiting for the next batch of pancakes to cook.

"Why don't you go have your coffee in the living room?" he suggested.

"That's okay," I said. "I can wait in here."

Then I heard a noise from the direction of the living room. I froze, suddenly suspicious. If the only people home were in the kitchen, who was out there? And why did my dad want me to go out there? Clutching my mug, I walked cautiously out of the kitchen. Someone was standing in the corner of the room near my project. But not just someone. "Jackson?"

He turned and smiled. "Good morning."

Despite our argument the day before, my heart still gave a little jolt seeing him. Then I realized that I hadn't even looked in the mirror when I went to the bathroom. I quickly set down my mug and ran my fingers through my sleep-styled hair. The good news was that I wasn't wearing embarrassing pajamas.

"What are you doing here so early?"

"Actually, I've been here all night."

The words made it to my ears, but then bounced right back out. "What? Why? And what are you doing with my project?"

The same excited smile he got when he talked about hockey players and NHL teams crossed his face. "You know how you couldn't get both the rotation and the lighting to work together?"

I frowned. "Yes."

"I found the problem."

Maybe it was because I hadn't had caffeine yet or maybe it was the words themselves, but my brain couldn't process that. "You what?"

"I figured out why it wouldn't work. It's a few lines of code that need to be fixed."

"But...but I've gone over every single line of code with a fine-tooth comb."

He waved me over to my laptop, which was resting on the coffee table, the cord running over the couch to the outlet on the wall. When I went over, the first thing he did was hold up his hands in innocence. "I haven't changed a thing. This is your original code."

Yeah. The code I'd struggled with for months. I was familiar with it. "Jackson, I've already tried everything. The project is due tomorrow. I'm not going to make it. I've accepted that."

"No offense," he said, "but you haven't tried everything. Look at these lines." He highlighted some of the code on the screen.

That was where everything seemed to fall apart, which I already knew. But I could humor him.

"Okay. I'm looking. But what am I looking at?"

"You're really close, but the problem is that you coded

them so that the lights and rotation work separately and together, or that's what you wanted to happen, right? But what you have to do is concatenate them using the logic that they fail if separate, but both execute if together."

My jaw dropped open. "How do you know that? And when did you learn the word 'concatenate?'" But before I could wait for an answer, my curiosity got the best of me, and I looked into the code. Maybe he was right. It was something I'd never tried before. Breaking the logic to require the two to be dependent never would have crossed my mind. I backed up the current code so I could start messing around.

Before I could get too absorbed, Jackson said, "I'll let you work. I have to get to practice soon anyway. If I miss another one, I'm pretty sure I'll be kicked off the team. But there's one more thing I wanted to show you." He tapped his phone screen a few times, then held it out to me.

On the screen was an email from the University of Southern California, thanking him for his application. A warm feeling started radiating out from my chest. I was pretty sure it was pride.

"You applied to USC?"

He shrugged. "The coach has been bugging me. Who knew a school in California would have a decent ice hockey program, right? Plus, it happens to only be thirty minutes away from one of the best astrophysics programs in the country."

Caltech. If I let myself dream, it would probably be my first choice. Well, my first realistic choice after Harvard and Princeton. And Jackson applied nearby. Jackson applied to a school. The pride in my chest grew. I threw myself at him in a hug he obviously wasn't prepared for, because he had to take a step back to steady himself. But then he hugged me back. Like my best friend. Like more than my best friend. Like everything could possibly be okay again.

I pushed back so I could see his face. "Wait. You did

that last night, too? Were you up all night? And how did you know all that coding stuff? I always *knew* you were smart. You should be the one submitting this project and going to Caltech, not me."

He laughed and held up a hand to stop me. "I'm not *that* smart. I did look into the code a lot, but I had to call in some help."

I narrowed my eyebrows. Who could he have possibly asked for help on this?

"Troy," he said, answering my unspoken question. "I FaceTimed with him about fifteen different times last night until we figured it out."

"Oh my gosh," I said. "You did that for me? Jackson... thank you. I..." I stammered. "I don't even know what to say."

"We didn't fix it for you. Wanted you to be the one to do that so you can take all the credit. I have no clue if this will actually work, but Troy seems to think it will, and if there's anyone in the world who can make it work, it's you. I have complete faith in you, Malina. And I have faith in us, too."

Those words made the warmth in my chest explode. I hugged him again, but this time he was ready for it. "I'm sorry I said all those things about you yesterday. I was upset about the interview."

He held me tighter. "I know. It's okay. And I'm sorry for the way I called you out, too. That wasn't cool."

"I think it was the nudge I needed." I let him go and said, "Honestly, I think missing that interview might have been the best thing that ever happened to me."

He grinned. "I agree. And I'm glad a good night's sleep changed your perspective on that." He checked his phone again. "I really have to get to practice. I'll come by after to see how it's going, okay?"

"Thank you, Jackson. For doing this. For believing in me."

"You're welcome. And thank you for pushing me."

"Thank Troy for me, too."

He waved me off. "You know he's into all of that kind of stuff. It was fun for him. The people I really need to thank are Krista and all of our teammates who have to deal with both of us on no sleep."

I laughed. "True."

He gave me a quick kiss, which I was glad was quick because I hadn't brushed my teeth yet. We said good-bye, and then he was gone.

Instead of sitting down with my cup of coffee, I sat in front of my computer and got to work.

"Pancakes are ready," Dad said, sticking his head into the living room.

"Can I get some in a few minutes? I have to do this while it's fresh in my mind."

"Sure. Did Jackson leave?"

"Yeah, he had to get to practice. Thank you for letting him stay here last night. What he did was…kind of amazing."

Dad gave a little smile. "You deserve amazing."

That comment gave me hope that we might be able to have the conversation we needed to have.

"Hey, Dad, can I talk to you for a second?"

He walked over and sat on the edge of the couch. "Sure. What's up?"

I took a deep breath. "I want to go to Caltech. Or maybe Rice or Berkley. I don't want to go to an in-state school, because none of them have the program I want. I don't want to go into business. I want to go into astrophysics. I know it's expensive and I know it's hard and competitive and it might not work out, but I feel like I have to try."

For a second, Dad didn't react at all. I wasn't sure what I expected. For him to blow up at me? To kick me out of the house? To give me a list of 432 reasons why this was the worst idea in the history of ever? But then he sighed. "Okay."

All of the defenses that I'd mentally prepared slipped away. *That* certainly wasn't what I'd expected.

"What? Did you say okay?"

"I did a lot of thinking last night. I don't think you would have missed that interview if the path I had you on was the path you actually wanted to go down. The bottom line is that I want you to be secure, Malina. I don't want you to have to struggle like I did, and I thought I found a solution for you for that. But the truth is that you have people in your life who are going to make sure you don't struggle. And the last thing I want is to stand in the way of your dreams. I've been doing that too much, and I'm sorry about that."

All of the oxygen left my lungs. Whoa. "Dad…that means the world to me."

He nodded once. "I may not be able to pay Caltech's tuition for you, and I may not be able to fix code for you, and I may not have a connection to get you a job in a field you really want, but I can support you. Be there for you. Which is what I'm going to do. No matter what."

I jumped up from my computer and wrapped my arms around him. "Thank you. You're the best."

He patted my back before letting me go. "I'm not the best. I'm not the one who stayed up all night studying code for you."

"That is awesome, but you're still the best."

"Good. Now get to work. I expect to see that up and running, or else no pancakes for you."

Chapter Twenty-Six

JACKSON

If I thought being nervous before a big game was bad, I was wrong. This was worse. *Way* worse. I was sitting in an uncomfortable, metal folding chair in a packed room, watching the STEM scholarship competition finalists give their presentations. I bounced my leg up and down, the same way I did in games when the backup goalie was in the net and I was on the bench with nothing to do but watch. The first few projects had been cool, but I'd barely been able to focus on them because I couldn't stop thinking about Malina. What was she doing backstage right then? Was *she* nervous? What would happen if her project didn't work the way she wanted it to?

When the applause for the project before hers died down, she took the stage. Her project was already on a table, tilted slightly so the audience could see, ready to go. In her hand, she held the phone with the app that controlled it.

My chest tightened. This was it. From the seat next to me, Izzy squeezed my arm hard enough to leave a mark.

Before Malina spoke, she made eye contact with me, smiled, and took a deep breath. "My name is Malina Hall. My main interests include space and coding, so I combined the two for my project."

She walked over to the table. She was wearing a dress and her hair was pulled back with a Hawaiian flower tucked behind her ear—probably something that Tutu had given her for luck. She looked amazing. Not only beautiful, but smart and confident and happy, too. Apparently Izzy and I were much more nervous than she was.

"This is a scale model of our solar system, made of glass. Within each piece of glass is an adjustable bulb. My project was to not only accurately rotate the planets around their axes and around the sun, but also to accurately scale and project the amount of light reflected by each planet, and to show how that light changes throughout each day and throughout the year."

There were a few murmurs in the crowd. This was the most complex project that had been presented so far. Now all she needed was for it to work. *Please let it work*.

She tapped her screen a few times. "When I turn on the app, time will start at the beginning of the day at the beginning of the year and move forward from there." When she tapped the phone again, the project lit up brilliantly with the sun at the center, and the planets began rotating in small circles around their axes and in larger arcs around the sun. Izzy and I both let out sighs of relief at the same time. Her grip on my arm loosened. The project was as beautiful as it was impressive, and the crowd chattered again.

"With the click of a button, I can fast forward to March, and you can see how the rotation and light change." She did, and the crowd clapped. She flushed adorably, but stayed focused on her project. "I can continue progressing through the year, until I end up right back in January."

She sped the project through the seasons, until Earth,

which was easy to pick out with all its blue and green, made its way back to its original location in reference to the sun. Then she looked out at the audience. "My calculations were based on each planet's albedo value. The rotation was scheduled based on standard orbital and rotation periods. I chose to work on this project because, like our own solar system, it's as much art as it is science. The beauty behind what we study sometimes gets left out of STEM, but I wanted to put it front and center. This project not only taught me about space and coding, but also about what it means to never stop learning and to never give up."

The crowed clapped again, and Malina took a little bow before returning backstage. My heart rate returned to normal. The project had worked. She'd made a great presentation. If she didn't leave with the scholarship money, she'd at least leave knowing that.

There were two more presentations after hers. "Neither of those were as good as hers," I whispered, leaning over to Izzy, who was sitting between me, Malina's parents, and Tutu.

"Absolutely not," Izzy whispered back. "Not that we're biased at all."

"Not at all," I agreed.

"Thank you, finalists," the MC said. He was wearing a tux, which seemed like overkill for a regional STEM competition, but whatever. "We'll let the judges deliberate for a few minutes. While we wait, please watch these messages from our sponsors and scholarship donors."

The lights dimmed and a screen came down. The crowd got restless, clearly more interested in the results than commercials, but thankfully it wasn't long before the lights came back on and the MC returned to the stage along with the finalists, carrying several envelopes.

"A big thank you to all of our sponsors. And now for the moment you've all been waiting for. Let's start with our honorable mention, earning a $500 scholarship. The honorable mention goes to…"

He dramatically opened the envelope. I held my breath. And released it when he read the name. Not Malina.

The process repeated when he got to third place. Not Malina.

Second place. Not Malina.

This was it. Either she won, or she got nothing. I didn't realize my knee was bouncing up and down again until Izzy reached over and pushed it down for me. It must have been driving her crazy.

"Sorry," I whispered.

"It's okay," she whispered back. "I'm nervous, too."

"And in first place, winning the grand prize, a four-year, $10,000 scholarship, is…"

The crowd was silent. Malina looked calm and collected even though I knew she couldn't possibly feel that way.

"Malina Hall!" the MC said.

My heart burst with excitement. Izzy and I jumped to our feet, whooping and hollering and making general fools of ourselves. I glanced toward Tutu, who was beaming with pride from her wheelchair, clapping and crying. Malina thanked the MC, accepted the giant cardboard check from one of the sponsors, and smiled for a few pictures. After one last thank you to all of the attendees and finalists, the room started to clear.

Malina was the last finalist off the stage. She walked toward our row, but she was walking to the opposite end where her parents were instead of to my end. I couldn't possibly wait another second to see her, so I jumped over the chair to the row in front of us, bypassed the Hall family, and jumped back into the right row in time to scoop her up in my arms and spin her around, causing her to drop the check.

"Jackson!" she said with a laugh.

I kissed her before putting her down. "I'm so proud of

you. I knew you could do it."

"I couldn't have done it without your help."

"We make a good team," I said, kissing her again.

"We do. Good thing we'll practically be neighbors in California."

Malina had been accepted to Caltech, and, with the help of the hockey coach, I'd been accepted at and committed to the University of Southern California.

"Good thing," I echoed.

"All right, all right, you've hogged her enough," Izzy said from behind me. "Give us a chance to congratulate her."

Reluctantly, I let Malina go and picked up the big check, with her name written in the "To" field. "I've never known anyone who got one of these in real life," I said.

"That's badass," Izzy said, squeezing by me to wrap Malina in a tight hug. "I'm so proud of you, you big nerd."

Malina laughed. "Thanks. I'm so happy. And so relieved it's over."

While Malina got hugs from Tutu and her mom, I examined the check with Mr. Hall. "So, does she just take this to the bank and cash it?" I asked.

Mr. Hall laughed. "I'll let you suggest that. And I'd like to be at the bank when you try." As soon as Malina was free, Mr. Hall was the last to wrap her in a hug. "You're amazing, Malina. You're going to make all of your dreams come true."

"That means a lot coming from you," she said. When her dad let her go, she had to wipe a few tears away. She cleared her throat. "So, what are we doing to celebrate?"

"I vote that the celebration includes food," I said right away.

She rolled her eyes at me, but she was smiling. "Of course you do."

I pulled her to my side and snuck in another quick kiss. "You love me."

"Yeah," she said. "I do."

Acknowledgments

It takes a village to make a book happen, and this one is no exception! First, a million thanks to Heather Howland. Four books later and I am still incredibly grateful that I get to work with you! Thank you for your expertise, time, and patience.

Many thanks to the entire Entangled team for your hard work on and support of my books. I couldn't ask for a better team!

Thank you to my family for providing endless encouragement. I love and appreciate all of you! Special thanks to Aunt Pat for always being the very first person to ask when my next book is coming out!

This book would not have been written without the #5amwritersclub. Thank you for the early morning friendship, virtual coffee and donuts, and making sure I don't turn off my alarm at 4:37 each morning!

To the Sweethearts of YA, thank you for all you do! I'm honored and thrilled to be part of such an amazing group.

To the writer friends who support me near and far, especially Kristi Kay, Julie C. Dao, Emmy Curtis, Kat Ellis,

Ralph Walker, Tif Marcelo, and Jess Skoog, thank you for the emails, tweets, texts, and words of encouragement that seem to come right when I need them most!

Last but certainly not least, thank you to readers for your support and for spending time in Jackson and Malina's world!

About the Author

Erin is a young adult author from North Carolina. She is a morning person who does most of her writing before sunrise, while drinking excessive quantities of coffee. She believes flip-flops qualify as year-round footwear, and would spend every day at the beach if she could. She has a bachelor's degree in mathematics, which is almost never useful when writing books.

Discover the **All Laced Up** *series...*

ALL LACED UP

Also by Erin Fletcher

PIECES OF YOU AND ME

WHERE YOU'LL FIND ME

Discover more of Entangled Teen Crush's books...

The Perfectly Imperfect Match
a Suttonville Sentinels novel by Kendra C. Highley

Pitcher Dylan Dennings has his future all mapped out: make the minors straight out of high school, work his way up the farm system, and get called up to the majors by the time he's twenty-three. The Plan has been his sole focus for years, and if making his dreams come true means instituting a strict "no girls" policy, so be it. Problem is, Dylan keeps running into Lucy Foster—needlepoint ninja, chicken advocate, and lover of mayhem. Every interaction sparks hotter than the last, but with Dylan's future on the line, he has to decide whether some rules are made to be broken...

Artificial Sweethearts
a *North Pole, Minnesota* novel by Julie Hammerle

It's not chemistry between Tinka Foster and Sam Anderson that made them agree to fake date. With her parents trying to set her up with an annoying pro-track golf student, and intentionally single Sam's family pressuring him to find a girlfriend, they could both use a drama-free summer. So it's not his muscular arms and quick wit that makes Tinka suggest they tell everyone they're both taken. Definitely not. And it's not butterflies that makes a kiss for appearances go on way too long. So there's no way fake couldn't be perfect.

Winging It
a *Corrigan Falls Raiders* novel by Cate Cameron

Natalie West and Toby Cooper were best friends growing up, on and off the ice. But when Toby's hockey career took off, their friendship was left behind. Now Natalie has a crazy plan to land her crush—and she needs Toby's help to pull it off. When Nat asks Toby to be her fake boyfriend, he can't say no. But Natalie's all grown up now, and spending time with her stirs up a lot of feelings, old and new. Suddenly pretending to be interested in her isn't hard at all...if only she wanted him and not his enemy.

CPSIA information can be obtained
at www.ICGtesting.com
Printed in the USA
FSOW04n2132221217
42665FS